KILLER COWBOY

BY
CARLA CASSIDY

MILLS &
BOON

First Published in Great Britain 2017
By Mills & Boon, an imprint of HarperCollins*Publishers*
1 London Bridge Street, London, SE1 9GF

© 2017 Carla Bracale

ISBN: 978-0-263-93041-2

18-0617

Our policy is to use papers that are natural, renewable and recyclable products and made from wood grown in sustainable forests.The logging and manufacturing processes conform to the legal environmental regulations of the country of origin.

Printed and bound in Spain
by CPI, Barcelona

Carla Cassidy is an award-winning, *New York Times* bestselling author who has written more than one-hundred-and-twenty novels for Mills & Boon. In 1995, she won Best Silhouette Romance from *RT Book Reviews* for *Anything for Danny*. In 1998, she won a Career Achievement Award for Best Innovative Series from *RT Book Reviews*. Carla believes the only thing better than curling up with a good book to read is sitting down at the computer with a good story to write.

Chapter 1

An elephant stood on Cassie Peterson's head. *Boom. Boom. Boom.* No, not standing. The darned behemoth was happily dancing on her skull, shooting out excruciating pain with each two-step.

She closed her gaping mouth and frowned at the nasty taste. Apparently, a carnival had also set up camp there and left behind a fuzzy tongue and the lingering taste of apple cider.

She cracked open an eyelid and groaned. No elephant in the bedroom. It was just a hangover from hell. How many glasses of Abe Breckenridge's famous apple cider had she drunk last night? And what on earth had he spiked it with?

Her headache continued to bang as she rolled over on her back and stared up at the ceiling. She couldn't remember the last time she'd suffered this kind of a hangover.

She also remembered very little of the last hour of the barn dance she'd thrown the night before. Despite her head pain a small smile curved her lips.

The barn dance had been a rousing success. Nearly everyone who lived in the small town of Bitterroot, Oklahoma, had attended.

Besides the fancy Western wear, some of the attendees had gotten into the Halloween spirit and dressed in costumes. The Croakin' Frogs band had provided the music and there had been plenty of eating, dancing and drinking.

Oh, she'd danced and drunk way too much. She needed to get out of bed. She had a barn to get cleaned up, but before that she hoped a long, hot shower would make her feel at least halfway human again.

With a groan she rolled out of the bed and padded into the adjoining bathroom. She stared at her reflection in the mirror and another low moan escaped her. Her curly blond hair was in tangles and mascara had moved from her lashes to form dark shadows beneath her eyes.

She looked like she'd been ridden hard and put away wet. "You wish," she said ruefully to the reflection and then turned her back and started the water for a shower.

Thirty minutes later Cassie headed down the stairs, feeling only marginally more human. Clad in a pair of her favorite jeans and a navy blue sweatshirt, she almost felt ready to face the day, although her head still banged with a fury, and she swore she would never drink apple cider again.

The scent of coffee wafted in the air and she assumed the ranch foreman, Adam Benson, had come in and was waiting for her in the kitchen.

She stepped into the bright, airy room and halted at the sight of Halena Redwing seated at the table with a cup of coffee in hand.

The old Choctaw woman wore a floral caftan from Cassie's closet and a cowboy hat and smiled with a knowing glint in her eyes. "You look like a woman who had too good a time last night."

Cassie moved over to the coffeepot and poured herself a cup and then joined Halena at the table. "I'm not sure my good time last night was worth my headache this morning."

"Greasy eggs, that's what you need." Halena got up and walked over to the refrigerator and pulled out the egg carton and a container of bacon fat.

"Ugh, that sounds awful."

"Greasy eggs and toast are great for a hangover." She leaned down and pulled out the skillet from a lower cabinet. "And I hope you remember that last night you said it was okay if I crashed out on your sofa and got something out of your closet to wear."

Cassie nodded and took a sip of her coffee. She vaguely remembered Tony Nakni, her ranch hand, asking her if Halena could spend the night because he and Halena's granddaughter had to get home early to take care of their precious little baby boy, whom they had left with a babysitter for the first time.

"Whose hat are you wearing?" Cassie asked in an attempt to get her mind off the pounding of her head and the slight nausea that arose from the scent of the melting bacon fat.

"Sawyer's." Halena turned from the stove and flashed Cassie a slightly naughty grin. "That boy is handsome as sin but he can't hold his liquor worth a damn. He passed out on one of the hay bales and I thought he might roll over and crush this hat, so I took it for the night."

Cassie couldn't help but smile as she thought of Sawyer Quincy. He was one of twelve cowboys she'd inherited when her aunt Cass had been killed in a tornado and left the huge ranch to Cassie six months before.

"Have any of the other men been in this morning?" she asked.

"Haven't seen hide nor hair of them." Halena cracked two eggs into the skillet.

Cassie wasn't surprised. She'd told the men to take the morning off, knowing that everyone would need some time to recuperate after last night's festivities. If they all felt as bad as she did, it might take a month for everyone to recuperate.

She sipped her coffee and stared out the window to the big barn in the distance. The party was supposed to be a turning point for her. She'd promised herself that once it was over she'd make a final decision about staying in Bitterroot or selling the ranch and returning to her old life in New York City. But this morning her head was much too fuzzy to even contemplate making a life-changing decision.

"Here you go." Halena set a plate in front of Cassie.

Cassie stared down at the toast and the two eggs with bright yellow, runny yolks and her stomach threatened to rebel.

"Eat up. Consider it medicine." Halena sat back down at the table.

"I'm more of an egg white kind of person," Cassie replied uneasily.

"That's just the big city in you doing the talking," Halena scoffed. "A little egg yolk never hurt anyone."

As Cassie forced herself to eat, Halena regaled her with stories from the night before. "I danced with every one of your cowboys. I even grabbed Dillon Bowie and forced him to two-step with me."

Cassie's heart jumped just a little at the mention of Bitterroot's chief of police. She had a bit of a crush on the dark-haired, gray-eyed man. But he'd given her no indication that he returned the feeling. In any case, it didn't matter if she was going to sell out and move on.

The back door opened and Adam Benson, the ranch foreman, walked in. "Good morning," he said and then smiled wryly. "Or is it?"

"She has a hangover, but she'll be fine once she finishes those eggs," Halena said.

Adam walked over to the coffeepot, poured himself a cup and then joined the two women at the table. "Heck of a shindig you threw last night."

"Remind me never again to drink Abe's special apple cider," Cassie replied.

"We all think his special ingredient is pure grain alcohol."

"Whatever it is, it's deadly," Cassie replied.

Adam turned to smile at Halena. "You were definitely the belle of the ball."

"I can't help it that men desire me and women envy me," Halena replied and tossed one of her long silver braids over her shoulder. Cassie would have laughed if she wasn't afraid her head might fall off.

"I'm assuming barn cleanup is on the agenda for the day," Adam said to Cassie.

She nodded and shoved her half-empty plate aside. "I'll walk through it this morning and see exactly what needs to be done to put things back to normal."

Halena got up and filled a large glass of water and then set it before Cassie. "Hydrate," she commanded.

Cassie smiled at the old woman. "Thanks, Halena."

"Thanks for what?"

"For taking care of a stupid woman who drank way too much last night."

"I think everyone drank too much last night," Adam replied.

Halena stood and took off Sawyer's cowboy hat. "I'd better get upstairs and change. Tony and Mary should be here anytime to pick me up. Will you see to it that Sawyer gets his hat back?"

"No problem," Cassie replied. "I was glad to see that the new hires seemed comfortable last night," she said when the older woman had left the kitchen. Two weeks ago she'd hired three new ranch hands.

"They're working out great and all the other men like them," Adam replied. "I was surprised to see some of Humes's men here last night. I wasn't aware you were going to invite them."

"I didn't." She paused to gulp down the glass of water and then continued, "They crashed. Thank goodness they didn't hang around too long." Raymond Humes owned the ranch next to hers, and his ranch hands were ill-mannered, mean-spirited men who enjoyed wreaking havoc anywhere they went, but especially on the Holiday ranch.

There was plenty of bad blood between her ranch and theirs. However, Raymond had made a generous offer to buy the ranch from her if she decided to sell.

She and Adam chatted for another half an hour and by then Halena had left, and the two of them got up from the table to head down to the barn.

"Halena's greasy eggs actually worked," she said as they stepped out the back door. "I'm feeling much better than I did when I first pulled myself out of bed." She drew in a deep breath of the clean country air and was happy to notice her headache had vanished.

The late-October sun was warm, although a cool breeze rustled through the last of the autumn leaves on the trees. New York's Central Park would be beautiful this time of year. She shoved the errant thought out of her head. She needed to stay focused on the here and now.

Still, there was beauty here, too. The sky was a gorgeous shade of blue, and the acres of land wore various shades of greens and browns like a patchwork quilt.

"I hope you keep feeling good after you see the condition of the barn," Adam replied ruefully.

"Oh, I'm expecting a mess," she assured him.

"One thing is for certain. People will be talking about the party for days to come. They'll gossip about who danced with whom and whose dress was too short or whose blouse was too tight."

"Uh-oh, that sounds like they'll be talking about me," Cassie said jokingly.

Adam's dark brown eyes were warm as he grinned. "You looked beautiful last night, as you always do." He quickly averted his gaze from her.

"Thanks, Adam," she replied. "Now, let's go see the damage."

As they took off walking, Cassie thought about the man next to her. She'd come to the ranch as a city girl, a struggling shop owner, who had dreams of being a famous artist. She hadn't known anything about cattle or ranches.

It had been Adam who had taken her by the hand and walked her through a learning process. He'd been so patient and kind and she never would have been able to manage running this place without him. She still learned something new from him every day.

He was also very easy on the eyes, with his dark brown hair and strong features. His shoulders were broad, his hips lean, and at times when he looked at her he made her feel like a desirable woman. But having a personal relationship with her ranch foreman wasn't a particularly good idea, and she just didn't feel that way about him, not that he'd ever made an advance.

They walked past the stables, and in the distance were the cowboy quarters, or the cowboy motel as they all called it. There were twelve small apartment units and in the back of the building was a large dining/recreation space.

Her aunt Cass Holiday had built an empire here, along with the help of twelve fiercely loyal cowboys. But this had never been Cassie's dream. She'd been here for almost six months and it still didn't feel like home.

As they approached the barn entrance she stifled a moan. The remains of the night's fun were already evident. Plastic cups were strewn around the area, along with paper plates and beer and other alcohol bottles.

"Doesn't anyone know how to use a trash bin anymore?" she said more to herself than to Adam.

"Hopefully knocking down the bandstand and picking up trash are the only real jobs needed," Adam replied.

They walked through the large double doors and

Cassie's nose was instantly assaulted by the lingering odors of body sweat, booze and barbecue.

Many of the bales of hay had been transformed into loose hay piles, and the orange and black streamers and Halloween decorations were either on the floor or tilted drunkenly on the walls.

A large tin tub held a few sad apples that bobbed listlessly on the small amount of water that remained, and a red-and-white woman's blouse hung on the arm of the blow-up skeleton.

"Uh-oh, who went home topless?" Cassie asked.

Adam grinned. "Amanda Wright, although she wasn't completely topless. She had on a red, white and blue sparkly bra last time I saw her."

"That must have been after I went to bed." Cassie leaned down and picked up a couple of beer cans and tossed them into a nearby trash barrel.

"Don't worry. By tonight we'll have this place back the way it belongs," Adam assured her.

She smiled at him. "I'm not worried. Aunt Cass was darned smart when she hired all of you."

A flash of pain darkened Adam's eyes. "She gave us all a chance at a new and good life. Most of us would have been dead or in jail by now if it wasn't for your aunt."

Cassie knew the story. When her uncle Hank had died of cancer, all the men who had worked on the ranch had walked off, convinced that a fifty-three-year-old widow would never be able to run the big place.

Cass, along with the help of a social worker, had

hired on a dozen runaway boys. That had been fifteen years ago and those boys had turned into fine, honorable and hardworking men who had been devoted to Cass.

"She loved all of you very much," Cassie said softly.

"She was the mother we never had. But now our loyalty is behind you."

Cassie knew that, and it only made the decision she had to make more difficult. She had no idea about the troubled backgrounds that had brought all the men here, but she knew they had embraced her as their own. The men who had been big Cass's cowboys had become hers.

She kicked at a pile of hay and frowned as her boot connected with something. "There's something under all this hay," she said.

She bent down and grabbed an armful of the hay and gasped as an arm appeared. "Oh, my God, there's somebody under here."

Adam quickly joined her and together they moved more of the hay, exposing Sam Kelly, one of the new hires. Cassie stumbled backward in horror.

It was obvious the man wasn't just dead drunk. He was dead. He lay on his back, his blue eyes unseeing, and a pool of blood surrounded the back of his head.

Shivers shot up her spine and bile rose up in the back of her throat. "Oh, no," she whispered faintly. Adam grabbed her and quickly guided her out of the barn.

"He's dead," she said and heard the beginning of hysteria in her own voice. She gulped in several deep breaths in an effort to calm herself, but it didn't work.

"Oh, my God, he's dead. He's dead, Adam."

Adam put his arms around her and she leaned weakly against him as tears burned hot at her eyes. How had this happened? Sam had been an affable young man who had instantly fit in with the other men.

What had happened to him? Dear God, who had done this to him?

"Cassie." Adam smoothed her hair away from her cheek. "We need to go back to the house and call Dillon."

Still she clung to him, the vision of Sam horrifying her as she thought of the seven skeletons that had recently been discovered beneath the old shed they'd torn down.

Fifteen years ago somebody had killed those seven young men with an ax or a meat cleaver to the backs of their heads, and those crimes had yet to be solved.

Was this the beginning of a new spree of death? Had the killer been inactive for all these years only to become active once again?

She hoped not. Maybe there was something beneath the hay that she hadn't seen, something sharp and deadly. Maybe Sam had fallen backward and hit his head on that something. But if he'd accidentally fallen, then who had covered his body with hay?

As Adam led her toward the house she could only pray that Sam's death was something far different than the evil that had taken place here so many years ago.

Chief of Police Dillon Bowie eased down in his office chair, pulled open his top drawer and grabbed the bottle of aspirin he kept there. He shook two pills out in his hand and chased them down with a swig of cold coffee.

It was his own fault he had a headache. He'd stayed too long at the barn dance, had drunk one too many glasses of whiskey and soda, and had burned with more than a little jealousy as he'd watched Cassie Peterson dance with practically every man in attendance.

Every man except you.

Of course he hadn't asked her to dance, even though he would have liked to hold her in his arms for just a bit. Since the minute she'd taken over the Holiday ranch, he'd entertained some lusty thoughts about the petite blonde, but they had remained just thoughts without any follow-through.

He leaned back in his chair and took another sip of his coffee. For the moment there was nothing pressing on his desk. The last six months had been a frenzy of crimes that had kept him busy and on edge. But nobody was in danger right now that he knew about, and he looked forward to just having some time to breathe.

While the fifteen-year-old crime that had taken

place on the Holiday ranch continued to torment him, he had no leads to follow at the moment.

He finished his coffee and then leaned forward and glanced through the reports that had come in overnight, seeing nothing earth-shattering. Most of the time crime-fighting in Bitterroot wasn't that challenging. There was an occasional domestic dispute or theft, and speeding down Main Street was a fairly common occurrence.

If things continued to stay quiet then maybe he could get some things done that he'd been putting off…like getting a haircut and doing a little maintenance work around his house.

A knock fell on his door and his dispatcher, Annie O'Brien, stuck her head in. "Just got a call from Adam Benson. They want you out at the Holiday ranch. One of the ranch hands is dead."

Dillon jumped out of his chair. So much for a minute to breathe. "Did he give you any other details?" he asked as the two of them stepped out of his office.

"Nothing," Annie replied.

Dillon walked into the squad room, where several of his men were seated at their desks. "Juan, Mike and Ben, we need to get out to the Holiday ranch. One of the cowboys is dead. You all follow me there."

Minutes later Dillon was in his vehicle with two patrol cars following behind him. What now? As if the mystery of seven dead young men on the ranch wasn't enough.

It was probably an accidental death with alcohol playing a big part. There had been a lot of people who had imbibed too freely at the barn dance the night before. He'd even thought he might have to arrest Amanda Wright for indecent exposure if her patriotic sparkly bra had followed the way of her blouse.

Cassie must be beside herself. She'd grown so close to all the men who worked for her. She'd certainly been horrified by the discovery of the seven skeletons on the property, as had the entire town.

What had happened on the Holiday ranch all those years ago, and who was responsible for the carnage? It was a question that would haunt Dillon until he had the answer, and he was convinced the answer lay with one of Cassie's cowboys.

He turned into the entry of the Holiday ranch and hoped that this was nothing more than a tragic accident. He parked close to the back porch of the house and Cassie and Adam walked out the door before he got out of his car.

Cassie looked achingly fragile and the sight of her tightened a ball of tension in his stomach. He left the car and approached the couple.

"He's in the barn," Cassie said. "It's Sam Kelly." Tears glistened in her bright blue eyes. "We think he was murdered."

Dillon's heart fell to the ground. "What makes you think that?"

Adam turned to Cassie. "Why don't you go back inside the house? I'll take Dillon down to the barn."

Cassie looked at Dillon for confirmation. He nodded. "Go ahead. I'll be in to talk to you later."

They both watched as Cassie turned and disappeared inside the house. When the back door closed, Adam turned back to Dillon.

"Cassie and I went to the barn earlier to see what kind of cleanup needed to be done after last night. When we found Sam, we came right back to the house. I called Sawyer and he's standing guard at the door to make sure nobody else enters the barn."

"Thanks," Dillon replied. Dammit, there was enough DNA in that barn to keep a lab busy for ten years. And that was only going to make a murder investigation even more difficult.

He and Adam headed to the barn with Dillon's officers following just behind them. Several of Cassie's cowboys were gathered around the barn doors, all of them wearing sober expressions and all of them a potential suspect if this was, indeed, a case of murder.

He didn't even want to think about the fact that everyone who had attended the barn dance would now be a suspect. "Adam will take me in. Everyone else stay out here," he said.

As the two of them walked into the barn, Dillon immediately spied the man half covered with hay. There was no question that he was dead.

"I need to get Teddy out here," Dillon said. Dr. Ted Lymon was the medical examiner and there wasn't much Dillon and his men could do here until Teddy arrived.

He made the call and then stepped closer to the body while Adam hung back. "This is how you found him?" he asked the ranch foreman.

"No. He was completely covered up in hay when we came into the barn. Cassie just happened to kick at the hay mound and realized something... somebody was beneath it." Adam grimaced. "As soon as we saw it was Sam we went back to the house to call you."

Dillon sighed. "Round up your men and make sure they're available for questioning later this afternoon."

Adam nodded and took the sentence as the dismissal it was meant to be. He turned and left the barn. Once again Dillon looked at the dead man.

Sam Kelly was a local. His parents had died in a car accident several years ago and since then he'd bummed around town doing odd jobs until he'd landed here on the Holiday ranch a couple of weeks ago.

He'd been a friendly young man, easygoing and seemingly without an enemy in the world. Yet somebody had killed him and buried his body with hay.

Dillon fought the impulse to lean down and gently brush the last of the hay off the man's face. He didn't dare touch anything until photos had been taken and Ted had done his job.

Whoever had done this had to have known his body would be discovered when the barn was cleaned up. On the portion of Sam's body that had been uncovered, Dillon saw no other wounds. The blood that had seeped out around the man's head tightened Dillon's gut.

Seven skeletons buried under the ground, each one showing deadly trauma to the back of the head. Now this, a man buried under hay with deadly trauma to the back of his head.

The similarities were hard to ignore, and Dillon's stomach churned with acid. Was it possible a serial killer had been dormant for all these years and now had become active again? Was the murder no more than a drunken brawl turned bad, or was it something far more insidious?

Chapter 2

Cassie made a fresh pot of coffee and then stood by the back door peering outside for what seemed like an eternity. She saw several more of Dillon's men arrive and then Ted Lymon pulled up in his black vehicle. Her heart ached as eventually Ted left with Sam's body.

Anger, heartbreak and a hint of fear all rolled around in her head and it felt as if it had been a hundred years ago that she'd awakened with her only concern being a hangover headache.

Her heart beat too quickly as she saw Dillon leave the barn and head toward the house. The man definitely stirred something inside her. At the moment she would love to lean into his broad chest and have his strong arms around her.

But of course that wouldn't happen. His strides were long and determined, and his mouth was a grim slash on his handsome face as he reached the back door.

His dark blue uniform shirt fit tight across his broad shoulders and the slacks fit perfectly on his long legs. Instead of an official hat, he wore a black cowboy hat.

Her head knew what he was going to tell her, but her heart wanted to deny it. She desperately wanted Sam's death to be a tragic accident, but the evidence said otherwise.

She opened the door for him. Despite the distress of the situation, she couldn't help that the familiar scent of his spicy cologne shot a hint of pleasant warmth through her.

"I made a fresh pot of coffee," she said. "Would you like a cup?"

"That sounds great," he agreed and sat at the table. He swept off his hat and placed it in the chair next to him.

She was acutely aware of his gaze on her as she poured them each a cup of coffee and then joined him at the table. She wrapped her fingers around her mug, suddenly cold again when she gazed into his troubled gray eyes.

"It's a murder case," he said.

His words didn't surprise her, but she couldn't help the small gasp that fell from her lips. "We'll know more after the autopsy," he continued. "Initially Teddy has declared the cause of death to be a sharp weapon slammed into the back of Sam's head."

"A sharp weapon?" Cassie licked her dry lips.

Dillon nodded, his dark, slightly shaggy hair gleaming brightly in the sunshine that danced through the nearby window. "Probably an ax."

"Like the others."

He paused to take a sip of the coffee then put his cup down slowly. "We can't be absolutely certain, but there's no way to dismiss the similarities." His gaze held hers intently. "Cassie, you need to face the fact that one of your cowboys might be guilty."

A rise of anger usurped the coldness inside her. "That's ridiculous. I know my men and my aunt Cass knew them. They're all good people who would never do something like this."

"I intend to question each of them as potential suspects."

She leaned forward in her chair. "You questioned them all when the seven skeletons were first found and nothing came of it. Maybe you should ask Humes's men what they were up to last night. They crashed the party and you know they've always been trouble."

There was no question that she lusted a bit after Dillon Bowie, but at the moment that emotion wasn't anywhere in her heart.

It was so much easier to embrace anger rather than to entertain her physical attraction to the chief of police, or give in to the tears that had threatened to fall since the moment she'd seen Sam's body.

She glared at him. "Why don't you leave my men alone? They've done nothing to make anyone believe that one of them is capable of murder."

"Calm down, Cassie."

She narrowed her eyes. "Has nobody in your entire life ever told you that telling a woman to calm down is like waving a red flag in front of an angry bull?"

His cheeks reddened slightly. "I'm not the enemy here, Cassie," he said softly. "Everyone who attended the barn dance last night is a potential suspect. In fact, what I need from you is a list of all the people who came to the party last night."

She frowned and leaned back in her chair, her momentary burst of anger gone. "You were here along with more than half the town." She sighed. "Okay, I'll do the best I can to come up with a complete list of names."

"I appreciate it. Now, tell me how Sam was working out here. I know he was a fairly new hire."

"I hired him on two weeks ago, along with Donnie Brighton and Jeff Hagerty. According to all the men Sam was fitting in just fine. Every time I saw him he had a cheerful smile on his face." She bit her bottom lip to keep her grief at bay.

"And nobody mentioned having a problem with him?"

She shook her head. "Nobody on this ranch. I don't know if he might have had issues with somebody in town."

"He'd moved in here when you hired him?"

"Yes, he moved into Tony Nakni's room after Tony moved in with Mary Redwing."

"Can you open his room for me?"

"Of course." Cassie got up and moved to the small built-in desk and opened the top drawer. "All of the men allow me to keep an extra key to their rooms for them in case of an emergency." She pulled out a key ring with an oversize charm of a huge pair of gemstone-red high heels. "I'll go with you."

She was grateful he didn't protest her presence as they walked out the back door. She was unsettled and didn't want to just sit inside the house with only her dark thoughts as company.

Grief for the young cowboy she was just getting to know weighed heavy in her heart, along with the uneasiness of knowing that last night a murderer had paid a visit to the Holiday ranch...to her ranch.

She had to double-step to keep up with the tall, long-legged man next to her. It had been months since the skeletons had been found on the property, and Dillon had been a familiar sight around the ranch and yet she really didn't know him very well.

All she knew for sure was there were times when his gaze lingered on her a bit too long, when wild butterflies shot off in the pit of her stomach. However, there were no butterflies right now as she glanced at his stern features.

They reached the cowboy motel where several of her men stood in a group outside their rooms.

"Hey, boss, are you doing okay?" Sawyer Quincy's copper-colored eyes held welcomed warmth as he gazed at her.

"Thanks, Sawyer. I'm okay," she replied.

"Hell of a way to end a party," Brody Booth said darkly. "Anyone tries to bash me in the back of the head with an ax, he'll get a bullet in his gut before he can even get close to me."

Cassie turned to Dillon in alarm. "Do you think the rest of my men are in danger?"

"There's no reason for me to believe that at the moment, but we've barely started this investigation," Dillon replied.

"You don't have to worry about us, Cassie. We all know how to take care of ourselves," Flint McCay assured her.

Cassie wanted to believe that, but yesterday she had believed that Sam Kelly could have taken care of himself. "I just want all of you to watch your backs," she said.

Aware that Dillon was waiting on her, she fumbled with the keys until she found the one that would unlock Sam's room. When the door was unlocked, she pushed it open.

Dillon stepped inside and she followed on his heels. The room was small, with just a twin bed against one wall and a chest of drawers on another. The closet door was open and the bathroom door was closed.

The sight of the pictures of his dead parents that Sam had hung on the wall made Cassie's heart cringe. The room was neat and clean and there appeared to be nothing out of place.

She remained just inside the door as Dillon pulled out drawers and examined each one. He then went into the bathroom and reappeared only a moment later.

"There doesn't seem to be anything here that will help me get to the bottom of things," he said and then heaved a deep sigh. "He had his phone with him when he was killed. Hopefully it will yield some sort of clue."

"He's with his parents now," Cassie said softly and then a sob escaped her.

Dillon turned to her, his gaze suddenly soft. "Go back to the house, Cassie." He placed a hand on her shoulder. "I've got interviews to do here and I'll check in with you later."

For a moment she wanted to lean into him and bury her face into the crook of his neck. She wanted him to wrap her in his arms and tell her that everything was going to be okay.

However, before she could follow through on the impulse, he removed his hand from her shoulder and stepped back. "I'd appreciate it if you could start on that list of people who were here at the party last night."

Cassie straightened her back and drew in a deep breath for strength. "I'll get right on it," she replied. "I'll see you later."

Heading back to the house, she wondered why

Sam's death had hit her so hard. She hadn't known him that well. Certainly it was always a tragedy when a person was murdered, but that didn't explain the utter devastation she felt.

An arctic chill swirled around inside her as she entered the house. She climbed the stairs and went down the hallway to her bedroom. What she really wanted to do was crawl back into bed.

Like a small child she wanted to fall into bed and pull the covers over her head and hide from all the evil she feared was coming her way. But she couldn't go back to bed. Instead she reached up to the shelf in the closet and tugged on the edge of a purple fuzzy throw blanket she'd put there when she'd first arrived at the ranch.

It came down along with several shoe boxes, framed photos and a handful of her aunt's clothes that Cassie had thrown on the shelf months ago.

"Damn, damn!" She rubbed her head where one of the picture frames had struck. She'd been telling herself she needed to clean out the closet shelf for months, but it wasn't going to happen right now.

She threw everything back on the shelf and then wrapped the throw around her shoulders and headed back downstairs. Instead of going to the kitchen table to start the list for Dillon, she collapsed on the sofa and pulled the throw more closely around her as the sobs she'd been holding back all morning released from her.

She cried for Sam Kelly, who had only been twenty-nine years old, and she cried because she didn't know what the future held. The only thing she knew for sure was that she was afraid.

The cowboy dining room was large. It not only held tables and chairs where the men ate their meals, but it also had an area with a television, sofa and several easy chairs where they relaxed on their time off in the evenings.

Dillon sat at one of the tables, waiting for another one of Cassie's cowboys to come in and be interviewed. His men were processing the barn and he'd already spoken to Sawyer Quincy and Mac McBride. Neither man had been able to shed any light on Sam's murder.

He didn't expect any of the men to give him something concrete, but he was hoping that if one of them lied to him then he'd pick up on the subtle signs.

He picked up his pen and tapped the end of it on the table as his head filled with thoughts of Cassie. She'd appeared so achingly fragile. She'd had nothing but drama since she'd taken over the ranch. As if unearthing the seven skeletons wasn't enough, her place had become a haven for people in trouble. Just last month a band of drug dealers had roared onto her land and shot up the place.

And now this.

He'd heard through the grapevine that she was considering selling out and heading back to New

York City. How could anyone really blame her? The big city would probably feel like a safe haven after everything that had happened here.

He looked up as Brody Booth walked in. The dark-haired, dark-eyed man wore an obvious chip on his shoulder as he threw himself into the chair opposite Dillon.

Bitterroot, Oklahoma, was a typical small town where everyone seemed to know everyone else's business, and gossip was as common as horseflies. But Dillon had never heard any gossip concerning the tall, well-built man facing him. Even the other cowboys who had grown up with Brody would admit that he was something of a dark enigma.

"I stayed at the party last night until around midnight and then I went to my room. I liked Sam okay, although I didn't really know him very well. He was a hard worker and I don't have any idea who might have killed him."

It was more words than Dillon had ever heard Brody speak. "Do you know if any of the other men had some sort of issue with Sam?" he asked.

"Not that I'm aware of, but I keep to myself mostly. Are you going to interview Zeke Osmond, Ace Sanders and Lloyd Green? They weren't even invited to the barn dance, yet they showed up anyway."

"I'll be talking to everyone who was at the party last night," Dillon replied. "I didn't see Humes's men starting any trouble while they were here."

Brody narrowed his eyes slightly. "Nobody ever

seems to actually see them doing anything wrong, but we both know they've been causing trouble for years, especially here on the Holiday ranch."

Dillon didn't reply. He knew Brody was right. "So, there's nothing you can add to help me solve Sam's murder."

"Nothing."

It was the same story with the six men he spoke to. Nobody knew of a reason anyone would want to kill Sam Kelly. The last time any of them had seen him was around midnight when he and Amanda Wright had bobbed for apples.

By the time Dillon finished with the interviews the dining room smelled of fried hamburger and onions. A glance at his watch let him know it was probably past time for the men to come in for their evening meal.

He got up from the table and walked around the wall that separated the kitchen from the dining room. Cord Cully, aka Cookie, frowned at his appearance.

The stocky man stood in front of the huge stovetop with a pancake turner in his hand. "I didn't go to the shindig last night so I got nothing to say to you." He flipped a burger over.

"If you weren't at the party, then where were you?"

He flipped another patty and then turned to gaze at Dillon. "I was in my house alone. I don't like parties. I prefer my own company to anyone else's.

Is that it? I have a meal to get to the table and you've already made it run late by almost an hour."

Cookie lived in a small cottage on the property. It was far enough away from the barn that nobody would have been able to tell if he'd been home last night or not.

"That's it for now," Dillon replied. Frustration burned in his belly as he left the dining room and headed back to the house.

Cookie was another dark horse that Dillon knew little about. He'd investigated the man when the skeletons had first been found. He knew that Cass had hired the man around the same time she'd taken in her runaway boys to work for her.

All Dillon knew for sure was the cook was originally from Texas and had no criminal background.

Dillon hadn't thought he'd solve the crime this afternoon, but he'd hoped for a smoking gun or at least a lead to follow up on, but so far he had nothing.

If he hadn't spent most of his time last night watching Cassie maybe he would have seen or heard something that might have led to a clue.

But he'd been captivated by the sight of the tight-jean-clad woman in the royal blue blouse that exactly matched her sparkling eyes.

She'd been the perfect hostess, making everyone feel welcome and checking to make sure the food table remained filled. Big Cass Holiday would have been proud of the niece who had inherited her ranch.

He knocked on the back door and Cassie's faint voice drifted out to him. He opened the door and stepped into the kitchen. It was a cheerful room with sunshine-yellow curtains at the window and a bright red and yellow rooster sitting in the center of the round oak table.

"In here, Dillon." Her voice came from the great room.

She was curled up in the corner of the large, over-stuffed sofa and wrapped in a purple blanket. Her eyes appeared to take on the hue of the blanket and instead of their normal sparkling bright blue they were the color of shadowed twilight.

A piece of paper and a pen rested on the coffee table, along with what appeared to be the last of a cup of hot tea.

She sat up and motioned for him to take a seat at the opposite end of the sofa.

"Did you solve everything?" She offered him a tired, sad smile that sliced directly through his heart.

"I wish," he replied. He eased down and immediately caught the scent of her. It was a hint of vanilla mingling with lilacs and as always it stirred something deep inside him.

He didn't want to talk to her about murder. Instead he'd rather have a conversation with her about her favorite song or color. He'd much rather hear her tell him about her dreams, or hear her musical laughter when he said something funny.

But there was nothing funny about their current situation and this wasn't a social visit.

"All the men cooperated with you?" she asked and allowed the blanket to fall off her shoulders.

"I spoke to six of them and they were all cooperative. I'll be back tomorrow to talk to the rest of them. I just wish somebody had seen or knew something about who killed Sam. According to several of them the last time they saw Sam at the party was around midnight when he was bobbing for apples with Amanda Wright."

"Where was her boyfriend?"

Dillon sat up straighter. "I didn't know she had a boyfriend."

"Butch Cooper. From the local gossip I think she's been dating him for about a month. I do know they arrived together last night."

Dillon frowned. Butch Cooper was a cowboy on Abe Breckenridge's ranch. He was a big guy and seemingly easygoing. But maybe he hadn't liked Sam and Amanda bobbing for apples together?

Cassie leaned forward. "You don't think…" Her voice trailed off.

"I think I need to speak to Butch. Do you have a list of names for me?"

She picked up a piece of paper. "I did the best I could, but I'm sure there are people who were at the party that I don't have down."

He stood and took the paper from her. "I appreciate you doing this much. Walk me out?"

"Of course." She rose to her feet and together they walked to the back door, where dusk had fallen.

She stepped out on the porch next to him. In the distance the barn was nothing more than a dark silhouette against the sky.

"I've got a couple of men there to guard the crime scene. Unfortunately it will be a few days before we're finished completely processing the barn. I'm sorry if that will inconvenience you."

"We'll be fine without using the barn for a while," she replied. She stared out into the distance and then shivered.

Dillon could stand it no longer. He reached out for her and she came willingly into his arms. He'd dreamed of holding Cassie many nights, but those dreams couldn't compare to the reality.

Her petite curves pressed against him as she raised her arms around his neck and clung to him. She released a small sob and he ran a hand through the softness of her blond curls in an attempt to soothe her.

"It's going to be all right, Cassie. I promise you I'm going to catch the person who killed Sam. You just have to stay strong."

"I'm so tired of being strong." Her breath was a warm caress in the crook of his neck. "I should just sell out and go back home."

Dillon dropped his arms from around her and took a step backward. "I wouldn't make any life-altering decisions right now, Cassie."

She wrapped her arms around herself and stared up at him. "I know it sounds crazy, but I feel like this town, this land, is telling me to get out." She drew in a deep breath and released it slowly. "It's just been a long day."

"Get some rest and I'll be back out here in the morning."

Minutes later Dillon was in his car and headed to the Breckenridge ranch to talk to Butch Cooper, but his thoughts remained on Cassie.

It had been years since he'd been drawn to a woman by some magnetic pull he didn't understand, but that was how he felt where Cassie was concerned.

Something drew him to her in spite of all the warning signals that went off in his head. He'd given away his heart once. He'd planned his future with his high school sweetheart, Stacy, and had begun to build dreams. However, life in Bitterroot—life with him—hadn't been exciting enough to keep her happy.

Dillon had a feeling Stacy and Cassie were cut from the same cloth and the last thing he wanted or needed in his life was a new heartbreak.

He tightened his fingers around the steering wheel and attempted to consciously shove thoughts of Cassie away. He had a murderer to catch and an old mystery to solve in order to finally silence the seven souls who haunted his dreams with the need for justice.

He leaned against the side of the house, his chest tight and his heart beating a hundred miles a minute. It was only natural that Dillon would give Cassie a hug under the circumstances. It didn't mean anything. It couldn't mean anything because Cassie belonged to him.

She didn't know it yet, but she'd belonged to him since the moment she'd arrived on this ranch. She was his angel, a woman who embodied everything he'd ever dreamed about.

In the months since she'd taken over the ranch she hadn't dated anyone. It was as if she was keeping herself pure and untouched just for him, and sooner or later he'd speak of his love for her, but not yet.

Thank God Dillon hadn't kissed her. He didn't know what he'd have done if the lawman's mouth had taken what belonged to him.

His heart slowed its beat and he left the side of the house, using the night shadows to stay concealed.

He'd loved and protected Big Cass Holiday when she'd been alive. His love for Cassie was different than the maternal love he'd had for her aunt. It was the love of a man for his mate and he intended to protect Cassie from anyone who might wrong or disrespect her.

That was why Sam had to die. He'd made a crude comment about wanting to get Cassie alone and naked in the hay. Sam had gotten what he deserved, as had all the other teenagers who'd come to work on the ranch, boys whom he'd had to kill so long ago.

The only thing that bothered him now was hearing Cassie say that she should sell the place and leave. Surely she was only feeling that way because of Sam's murder. She wouldn't really follow through. It would be a betrayal to her dead aunt, but more important it would be a betrayal to all the men who worked for her.

He refused to believe that she would make such a decision. She belonged here and eventually she'd realize that her future was with him right here on the Holiday ranch.

Chapter 3

Cassie sat at the kitchen table with a cup of coffee in front of her. Dawn light was just peeking over the horizon and she'd been awake for hours.

It had been about three when she'd awakened from a horrible nightmare. An ax-wielding dark shadow had been chasing her around the house and she'd jerked awake just before he caught her.

For the next couple of hours she'd tossed and turned in an effort to go back to sleep, but she'd finally given up and gotten out of bed. She'd showered quickly, and then had dressed in a pair of jeans and a light pink sweatshirt and had come downstairs.

Now, instead of ax murderers, her head was filled with thoughts of Dillon. Despite her sadness over Sam's murder, she'd liked the feel of Dillon's arms around her the night before. The scent of his cologne had become familiar to her and as she'd buried her head against him, the fragrance had comforted her. And stirred more than a little bit of desire in her.

She'd wanted him to kiss her, and yet she knew it was foolish even to think about a romantic relationship with anyone here in Bitterroot. She didn't know if she intended to stay here or go back to her old life and her dreams in New York City.

She leaned forward and took a sip of her now-cold coffee. The big two-story house was silent and she'd never felt so unsettled and so alone.

She'd arrived on the ranch in the spring with her best friend and partner, Nicolette Kendall, and her young son. Nicolette and Sammy had taken to ranch life as if they'd been born here.

It hadn't taken Nicolette long to catch the eye of Lucas Taylor, one of the cowboys who worked for Cassie. They were now happily married and Cassie was miserably alone.

It wasn't that Cassie wasn't happy for her friend. She was thrilled that Nicolette had found true love and happiness. Cassie just wished she knew where she belonged in the grand scheme of life.

Was it here on this ranch in this small town, or did her destiny lay in New York City where she could pursue her dreams of being a famous artist?

She'd love to pick up the phone and call Nicolette, but she knew her friend would be busy with her family. Cassie wished she had the kind of relationship with her mother where she could pick up the phone and get her guidance. Her parents had pretty well written her off when she'd dropped out of college and refused to go to law school and join the family legal firm.

She cast her gaze out the window, unsurprised to see Adam walking toward the house as the sun rose above the horizon. He'd be startled to find her up and dressed and with the coffee already made.

It was their habit that he let himself inside in the mornings, made the coffee and then waited for her to join him for the daily ranch update. Apparently, even a brutal murder didn't change the routine on a ranch.

Morning greetings were exchanged and then Adam joined her at the table with a cup of coffee. "How are you doing?" he asked.

"Okay, I guess," she replied. "Although I'm still horrified and saddened by Sam's death."

"We all are. Dillon said he'd be back here around eight this morning to talk to some more of the men. He's wasting his time. He won't find his answers here."

"I told him as much yesterday." She got up from the table to get a fresh cup of coffee, fighting against the memory of being held far too briefly in the lawman's arms.

"I still think he'd better be looking hard at Butch Cooper," Adam said when she was seated once again. "Amanda was flirting pretty hardcore with Sam at the party and Butch might be an easygoing guy, but he didn't look all that happy."

"I'm sure Dillon is going to explore all the possibilities."

"Yeah, I just wish he'd stop focusing so much attention on us." Adam took a sip from his cup and then guided his attention out the window. "Anything that happens around here, he's always quick to interrogate all of us."

"He's just doing his job, Adam."

He focused his gaze back on her and smiled. "I know. It's just frustrating. He's had his eye on us since those skeletons were discovered. Whatever happened to those teenagers happened before we all got here. All the men who grew up here on the ranch are good, solid people. You should know that by now."

She returned his smile. "Believe me, I do."

For the next twenty minutes he filled her in on the ranch business. Over the past six months Cassie had learned more about cattle than she'd ever wanted to know, but this was her life at the moment.

As Adam droned on about plans for the upcoming winter months, Cassie's mind remained on the murder and what it meant for her future.

There was no way she could sell the property and leave for New York right now. Legally she was as much a suspect as anyone else that had attended the party, although surely nobody would really believe she'd had anything to do with Sam's murder.

"Cassie?"

Adam's voice pulled her out of her own head. "Sorry, what did you say?" she replied.

"I know you have a lot on your mind, so I'll just get out of your hair and get to work." He stood, drained his coffee cup and then carried it over to the sink. "I'll check in with you later in the day after Dillon has conducted the rest of his interviews."

"Thanks, Adam." She didn't bother getting up. Once Adam was gone she remained at the table until Dillon's car appeared in the drive by the back door.

As he stepped out of the car, the hint of heat she always felt when around him whispered through her. He approached the house and knocked on the back door.

"It's open," she yelled. "We've got to stop meeting like this," she said when he stepped into the kitchen.

"Then stop having murder victims on your property," he replied.

"Trust me, I'd love to stop." She motioned to the coffeepot. "Help yourself."

"Thanks, but I'm good. I just wanted to let you know I'll be around here most of the day."

"Did you find out anything yesterday that might help you solve this?"

His eyes were steel-gray and troubled. "Cassie, we aren't going to solve this in a day. We have a barn full of people to interview and little physical evidence."

"I know." She blew out a sigh. "People were already talking about this land being damned because of the seven skeletons that were found here."

"Your land isn't damned and you know I've been

working as hard as I can to solve the mystery of those skeletons. Unfortunately, it's difficult to solve a fifteen-year-old crime where I only have one potentially important clue."

Cassie straightened in her chair. "An important clue? Tell me, Dillon, what is it?" Was it really possible that he could solve the crime? Could he finally give peace to the seven young men who had been murdered?

Dillon frowned and shifted from one foot to the other, obviously contemplating whether to tell her or not. "You can't share this with anyone," he finally said.

"I promise," she replied.

"It's a man's ring. When we were excavating the graves, in the bottom of one was a gold ring with an onyx stone. I believe it slipped off the killer's finger when he was burying one of the bodies."

"Was there any DNA on it?"

"Whatever was there was so contaminated nothing was usable." He took a step toward the back door. "I've got to get to work. I'll talk to you later this afternoon." With that he turned and left the house.

Through the window Cassie watched him walk toward the barn. She couldn't help but notice how good his butt looked in his uniform pants. He was definitely hot.

She'd never heard any gossip about who he dated, and this was a small town that loved their gossip. All she really knew about Dillon Bowie was that he was well respected by everyone in Bitterroot and lived on a small farmstead on the other side of town. And she had the hots for him.

Restless energy surged up inside her. She got up from the table and put the coffee cups in the dishwasher. The ring of the doorbell whirled her around.

Who on earth could that be? She didn't think anyone had ever come to the front door since she'd moved in. Everyone used the back door when they visited.

She hurried through the great room and into the smaller, more formal living room, where she could see through a side window that Raymond Humes stood on the porch.

She stifled a groan. That man was the last person on earth she wanted to see this morning. She opened the door and greeted him through the screen. "Good morning, Mr. Humes. What can I do for you?"

The silver-haired thin man smiled, the gesture doing nothing to warm the cold of his close-set dark eyes. "It isn't what you can do for me. It's about what I can do for you. May I come in?"

Cassie hesitated. She knew why he was here. The seventysomething-year-old man was like a vulture sensing death and waiting to capitalize on any weakness. She finally opened the screen door to allow him inside.

She refused to lead him into the heart of the house and instead gestured to the small floral sofa just inside the front door. She sat on the edge of the wing-backed chair facing him.

He swept his dusty brown cowboy hat off his head. "I was sorry to hear about poor Sam's unfortunate demise," he began. "You do realize this is only going to add a new blight on this ranch that will make it even more difficult for you to sell."

"I've told you several times I'm not ready to sell at this point in time," she replied.

"You aren't going to get a better offer than mine," he said with a confidence that irritated her.

"I'm not interested in any offer right now and did you know some of your ranch hands crashed my barn dance the other night?"

Raymond chuckled. "Hardly a crime. I found it hard to believe that you wouldn't invite me and my men to the shindig being that we're neighbors and all."

"Your men and mine aren't really friendly," she replied as she stood.

"I've never understood that," he said in bemusement.

She understood. According to her men, Humes's ranch hands had stolen cattle, set malicious fires and done sundry other things to her ranch.

"I've got a lot of things going on right now, Mr. Humes. I appreciate you stopping by, but I'm not interested in any offer you might make me on this place." She glanced pointedly at the door.

Raymond laughed once again as he rose from the sofa. "Sooner or later you'll be interested. I'm the only person around these parts who has the kind of money you'll want to rid yourself of this one-horse town and get back to New York City, where those fancy jeans of yours belong."

"I'll keep that in mind," she replied.

She breathed a sigh of relief when he walked out the door. He was probably pleased that another murder had taken place on her property. He probably thought this newest tragedy would make her desperate to sell out to him and leave Bitterroot.

She had to admit there was a part of her that would like to cut and run. However, selling out to Raymond Humes would be such a betrayal to Aunt Cass, who had left her the ranch.

More important, it would be a huge betrayal to the men who worked here, men who embraced her as their own the minute she'd stepped into her aunt's very large shoes.

And one of them might be a killer.

The words jumped unbidden into her head. No, there was no way Dillon or anyone else could ever make her believe that. She refused to believe that for the last six months she'd been living here with a vicious killer. Her cowboys were good, kind and hardworking men.

Still, a faint chill accompanied her as she locked the front door and then returned to the kitchen.

It was just after four when Dillon finished interviewing for the day. He'd spent most of the morning inside the barn with a couple of his best men, seeking anything that might be a clue. It had been a fruitless search.

Finally, after noon he pulled in three of the last six cowboys to talk to. He'd hoped to get something, at least a little nugget of information that might move the case forward, but that hadn't happened.

Over and over again he heard that Sam had fit in with them all just fine, that nobody had seen anything at the party indicating a problem between the dead man and anyone else other than Butch.

There were still many avenues to explore, but Dillon felt in his gut that the answers not only to Sam's murder, but also to the murders that had taken place years ago, lay right here on the Holiday ranch.

As he headed to the house a weariness weighed heavily on his shoulders. It was the same disillusionment that had been with him since the day the seven bodies had been unearthed.

Dillon considered himself a good lawman, but the seven unsolved mysteries had left him feeling inadequate. It was an emotion that brought up old, bad memories. He shoved them aside as he reached the back door.

He'd been kicking himself all day for sharing with Cassie the information about the ring that had been found in the grave. He should have never confided in her. While he trusted that she would keep the information to herself, it had been unprofessional of him to tell her.

But he'd wanted to give her just a small nugget of hope that he would get to the bottom of things. He'd wanted to do something to alleviate the shadowed darkness in her eyes.

He knocked on the back door and Cassie answered. "Come on in," she said, gesturing him into the kitchen that smelled of spicy meat cooking.

"Something smells good," he said.

"Taco pie. Halena Redwing taught me how to make it. Why don't you have some with me? I've already made a salad, and the pie will be ready in minutes."

"Oh, I don't want to impose…" he began.

"Dillon, please. It's no imposition at all. Besides, I absolutely hate to eat alone."

There was something slightly desperate in the depths of her lovely eyes. It probably wasn't a good idea for him to spend any time with her, especially alone. "I skipped lunch and taco pie sounds delicious," he heard himself say despite his internal dialogue.

She flashed him a grateful smile. "Then sit and relax and I'll just get the dishes on the table."

"What can I do to help?"

"Don't talk about murder or my men while we eat." She pointed to a chair.

"I can do that," he agreed and sat. He'd talked and thought about murder enough for the day. The taco pie smelled delicious and Cassie looked charming in a pair of fancy jeans that hugged her slender legs and a pink sweatshirt that made her eyes appear even more blue than usual.

He remained silent while she placed plates and silverware on the table. As she bent over to get the taco bake out of the oven, he couldn't help but notice her figure. She was a petite woman, but perfectly proportioned.

Cassie Peterson could definitely be a threat to his mental well-being if he allowed it. She was the first woman to tempt him since Stacy had walked out on him almost five years ago.

It's just a quick dinner, he told himself. No threat there. It would be nice not to talk about murder or potential suspects for the duration of the meal. He just wasn't sure what they might talk about. In the past every time he'd spoken to Cassie it had been because something bad had happened on her ranch.

Something bad had happened now, but he was almost grateful she didn't want to chew on it over dinner.

Minutes later she had the meal on the table and gestured for him to help himself. "Why did you skip lunch? You know you would have been welcome to eat with the men. Cookie always makes plenty of food."

He didn't want to tell her that he wasn't at all sure he'd be welcome in the dining room. Between yesterday and that afternoon he'd grilled most of her men pretty hard. "I was busy in the barn and lost track of time," he replied. He ladled a portion of the pie from the dish onto his plate.

"The weather was certainly nice today," she said.

"Autumn is my favorite season," he replied.

"Mine, too." She smiled, as if pleased they'd found some common ground.

He focused on his plate and tried to ignore the

small burst of heat her smile had sparked in the pit of his stomach. He took a bite of the taco pie and then gazed at her once again. "This is delicious. You're obviously a good cook."

She laughed, the sound musical and pleasant. "Not really, but I'm trying. Halena has given me a ton of her recipes, and she's a good cook. There are a lot of Aunt Cass's recipes here, too. I've realized in the last couple of weeks that cooking and baking might be a great stress reliever if I learn how to do it right."

"Maybe I should take it up," Dillon said drily.

"You don't cook?"

"Most of my meals are eaten at the café. I work so much that it's just easier to eat out."

"All work and no play?" She took a bite of her salad and held his gaze.

Oh, he'd like to play right now. He'd like to capture her cupid lips with his and… Crap, the stress of these cases was definitely getting to him.

"No play," he replied more curtly than he intended. She looked down at her plate and he instantly felt guilty for his sharp tone. "I heard through the grapevine that you're an artist."

She looked at him once again. "I like to paint."

"Watercolor or oil?"

Her eyes lit up. "Right now I'm doing oil paintings with Western themes. I have an arrangement with Mary Redwing. She's got a couple of them up on her website for sale."

"From everything I've heard Mary has a solid

business." The Native American woman sold hand-made baskets, pots and other items inherent to her Choctaw culture while her grandmother, Halena, sewed traditional dresses to sell.

"Have you always liked to paint?" He felt himself begin to relax for the first time in weeks.

"Always. All I ever dreamed of was becoming a famous artist. That's what I was working toward before I came here. I owned a small shop that sold my artwork along with some other items."

"Was it successful?"

She hesitated before replying and her eyes darkened slightly. "I was struggling to make ends meet. I think with more time and money it might have been a real success. I never dreamed I'd wind up on a ranch in Oklahoma."

"Were you close to your aunt Cass?"

"Not really, although I was named after her. She came to New York a couple of times to visit my parents and when I was about ten we came out here to visit. But that was about it. That's why I was so surprised when she left me this place." She paused to take a drink of water and then continued, "Aunt Cass was kind of the outcast of the family. My parents are very New York. They're both criminal defense lawyers and extremely driven."

For the next half an hour they ate and she talked about her parents and her life before Holiday ranch. He laughed as she related stories about quirky characters who had come into her shop.

"You know, Bitterroot isn't without its own quirky characters," he said.

"I already know that Halena loves to wear funky hats and occasionally pinches some cowboy's butt."

He laughed. "That she does, but I'll bet you didn't know that Leroy Atkinson has his entire house lined inside with aluminum foil so space aliens can't see him or hear his thoughts. He also believes aliens visit his ranch on numerous occasions."

Her eyes lit with suppressed laughter. "Is that for real or are you making it up?"

"I don't make stuff up," he replied. "About twice a month Leroy calls me out to his ranch to see evidence that a spaceship has landed on his property. I never see anything other than some tamped-down grass where a cow rested through the night. Actually, my parents lived next to Leroy when I was a kid. Leroy was like a second father to me. He calls me out to his ranch because he's lonely."

"That's sad," she said. By this time their plates were empty. "Would you like an after-dinner cup of coffee?" she asked. She stood and a spark of fading sunlight danced in the strands of her curly blond hair.

The desire to touch the soft-looking curls itched his palms. "Thanks, but I should probably be on my way." He needed to get out of here. Spending time with her had been far too pleasurable.

He got up from the table. "Thanks for the great meal."

"Thank you for sharing it with me. Sometimes this big old house gets a bit lonely," she replied.

He headed toward the back door, needing to escape her. Without the smell of the food, he became acutely aware of her lilac and vanilla scent that wafted in the air. The kitchen suddenly felt smaller, more oppressive.

He turned to tell her goodbye and she was right there, standing mere inches from him. Her lips were slightly parted as if anticipating a kiss, and even before he recognized his own intention, he drew her to him and covered her mouth with his.

Her lips were welcome heat and sweet softness. Somewhere in the back of his mind he thought she'd pull away, but instead she leaned into him and opened her mouth a little more in invitation. Desire suffused him as he deepened the kiss, and their tongues swirled together in a heated dance.

He might have kissed her forever if she hadn't released a throaty little moan. It made him want to pick her up and carry her into the house and to the nearest bedroom.

And that emotion was what shot some sense through his head. He dropped his arms to his waist and stepped back from her. "Sorry, that was a huge mistake."

"A mistake?" Her winsome blue eyes searched his features in puzzlement. "Why was it a mistake?"

He shoved his hands in his pockets to stymie them from reaching out for her again. "I shouldn't have kissed you because before this case is over I think you're probably going to hate me."

"Why would I have a reason to hate you?"

"Because I believe one of your cowboys is guilty of not only killing Sam, but also those seven young men who were found under the shed. One of them is guilty and I'm not going to stop until I prove it."

He didn't wait for her response, but instead turned and went out the door.

Chapter 4

Cassie was once again seated at the kitchen table the next afternoon when Dillon's car pulled into the drive. She sat up straighter in anticipation of him coming inside, but he headed straight to the barn.

She tamped down her disappointment that he hadn't come in to say hello. He wasn't here to visit, she reminded herself. He had a job to do, but there was no question that his kiss had both thrilled and confused her.

That kiss. Even now just thinking about it made her toes curl. She'd spent half the night replaying it over and over again in her head. Between the kiss and his parting words she felt as if he'd caressed her heart and then slapped her upside the head.

Her phone had rung for most of the day, neighbors and friends checking in with her and wanting to know the latest on the murder investigation. She told them nothing because she knew nothing except that Dillon was convinced one of her men was a monster.

Today she couldn't even be too mad at him for his beliefs, despite the fact that she found the idea completely ludicrous. That didn't take away from the fact that his kiss had shaken her to her core.

It had been over two years ago since she'd had a relationship with a man. She and Mark had dated for eight months before he'd finally broken up with her. She'd been surprised to discover that she'd actually been relieved by the split.

At the time she'd been consumed with her shop, working long hours there, and when she wasn't behind the counter she was in her studio apartment painting. She hadn't put in the time or energy to make her relationship work.

What they had shared was basically a physical thing without any real emotional tie. At the end he'd wanted more from her, but she hadn't been willing to take it any deeper.

She cast another glance out the window. It was time to stop sitting around and brooding and instead she went to work fixing a big pot of chili. The day had been gray and cool, perfect for chili with corn bread.

As she worked she occasionally drifted to the window to peer out. Dillon's car was still in the drive but the only people she saw were two of her men on horseback in the distance.

Maybe he'd stay for dinner again tonight and maybe he'd kiss her again. Probably not, since he'd told her their first kiss was a mistake. It certainly hadn't felt like a mistake to her. It had felt wonderfully right.

What did she think she was doing, wishing for another kiss from him? The last thing she wanted was a relationship that might make it even more difficult for her to make the decision to stay or leave here.

And she had to make that decision within the next few weeks. If she was going to sell the ranch and head back to New York City she wanted to do it before the first snow flew.

She jumped as a knock fell on the back door. She turned around from the stove to see Sawyer standing on the small stoop. She gestured him inside with a smile. Sawyer Quincy was one of her favorites of all the men. The tall, lean man had an easy way about him and was always quick to laugh.

"I was just on my way into town to pick up some things for Cookie and I thought I'd check in and see if you needed anything," he said.

This wasn't the first time Sawyer had gone out of his way to do something nice for her. "Thanks, Sawyer, but I think I'm good for now."

"That chili definitely smells good," he replied and gestured to the pot simmering on the stovetop.

"Thanks, it just felt like a chili kind of day."

"Winter will be here before you know it."

"Don't remind me." She picked up a large spoon and stirred the chili.

"We'll get through winter, and we'll get through what's happening right now."

She placed the spoon on a spoon rest and released a deep sigh. "How are things going today? I haven't spoken to Dillon yet."

Sawyer's eyes flashed darkly. "He's questioning all of us all over again. It's like he's just looking for one of us to make a mistake or something. Oh, well, I'd better get going. Cookie will pitch a fit if I don't get back with his stuff as soon as possible."

"Get out of here," she replied with a laugh. "I wouldn't want to be responsible for one of Cookie's temper fits." With a goodbye, he walked out the back door and Cassie returned to the counter to make the corn bread.

She wouldn't put it past Raymond Humes to arrange for one of his men to murder one of hers just to stain the ranch reputation and make her more desperate to sell. She only hoped Dillon was questioning him and his men as hard as he was hers.

It was just after six when Dillon knocked on the back door. The kitchen smelled of the chili and corn bread, and Cassie couldn't help the little bit of anticipation that danced in her stomach as she thought about them sharing another meal.

"I just wanted to let you know I'm heading back into town," he said.

"How about a bowl of chili before you take off? I was just getting ready to sit down to eat and there's plenty."

He hesitated and his gaze held hers for a long moment. In the depths of his eyes she thought she saw a spark of something that made her breath quicken as a wave of heat shimmied through her.

He blinked and broke the eye contact with her. "Thanks for the offer, but I really should get going. I've got some other people I want to talk to before I call it a day." He sidled toward the door as if eager to escape.

She tamped down her disappointment. "You'll keep me informed if you find out anything that will solve the murder?"

"Of course," he replied and still didn't look at her. Instead he appeared to find the rooster in the center of the table utterly fascinating.

"Did Sam's phone tell you anything?" she asked.

"Nothing worthwhile. So far I haven't learned anything that would move the case forward."

"Did you talk to Butch?"

"I did, and I believe he's a dead end and had nothing to do with Sam's death." He finally looked at her once again. "I'll see you sometime tomorrow."

"Then I'll just say good-night," she replied.

He nodded and went out the door.

Despite the hour an early twilight had fallen. Cassie turned on the kitchen light and ladled up a bowl of chili for herself.

If he hadn't kissed her so thoroughly the night before she wouldn't be feeling so disappointed that he hadn't stayed to eat with her tonight.

The kiss had scrambled her brains and made her

want more despite her reluctance to form any kind of a relationship with any man.

It wasn't just the very hot kiss. He'd been so easy to talk to and she'd enjoyed their conversation and the laughter they'd shared the night before. She'd been intrigued by Dillon Bowie since the moment she'd met him, and eating dinner with him last night had only made her more interested in him.

Maybe it was a good thing he hadn't stayed to eat with her. The chili was overspiced and the corn bread was burnt on the bottom. Another failed attempt at cooking, she thought with chagrin.

After eating her dinner she cleaned up the kitchen and then wandered restlessly around the great room, the hours before bedtime stretching out empty and silent before her.

It was just after seven when she decided to go out to one of the small sheds and get some more of her aunt Cass's journals that were stored there. She'd found the stash of journals several months ago and had been reading them off and on since then. She'd read all the ones she'd brought into the house and tonight seemed like a good time to read a new one.

She grabbed a jacket off a hook by the kitchen door and pulled it on, then retrieved a flashlight from beneath the kitchen sink.

The night appeared darker than usual without the benefit of any moonlight or star shine. She clicked on her flashlight and headed toward the shed in the distance.

She found it oddly comforting to see the lights

shining outside the windows in the cowboy motel. They were like beacons of comfort and reminded her she wasn't all alone on the property.

The shed was a fairly small wooden structure and inside were things her aunt had stored. Along with the journals there were boxes of old kitchen utensils, Christmas decorations and a huge box of brightly decorated ceramic Easter bunnies.

She released the padlock and pulled the door open, her flashlight beam dancing across the boxes. Thankfully, the one she wanted was on top and easy to get to.

Opening the box, she used her light to grab a handful of the journals that were on top. The shed door slammed shut behind her. She whirled around with a surprised squeal.

Had the wind suddenly picked up and blown the door closed? Impossible. Her heart nearly beat out of her chest. The door was heavy and only a tornado-like gust could have shut it.

She ran to the door and tried to open it, but there was no give. An edge of panic crawled up her throat. She used her shoulder to push against the door, but it refused to open.

Somebody had shut the door and locked her inside. Oh, God, who had done this and why? Full-blown panic grabbed her by the throat.

She dropped the journals on the floor and banged on the door with her fist. "Hello? Somebody help me! I'm in here!" She screamed the words over and over again.

All the men would be in their rooms by now, too far away to hear her cries for help. There was only one person who might hear her and that was the person who had locked her in.

She froze, her heart racing even faster. Was he standing just outside the door right now? Gloating as he heard her panicked screams? Was he going to listen to her terror and then open the door and…? A vision of Sam dead in the hay filled her mind. She nearly dropped her flashlight as an icy chill suffused her. Tears burned at her eyes, half blinding her in the semidarkness.

She banged on the door and began to scream once again in wild hopes that somebody would hear her, praying that somebody would save her. There was no point to stay silent whether the person who'd locked her in was just outside or not.

She didn't know how long she banged and yelled before she heard a voice. "Cassie?" The faint, familiar voice drifted through the door.

"Adam? I'm in here. Please, open the door," she cried. She heard the lock being removed, and as the door opened a sob of relief escaped her.

"What happened?" Adam asked as he reached for her. "How did you get in there?"

"I came out here to get something and the door slammed behind me and I couldn't get out and…" She broke off as she began to cry.

"Let's get you to the house," Adam said.

She nodded and reached down to grab the journals. She was still weeping as Adam threw a comforting arm around her shoulder and led her toward the house.

When they got inside she collapsed on the sofa. "What were you doing outside?" she asked as her tears slowly subsided.

"I always do a check on things around the ranch in the evenings," he replied. His eyes were dark and filled with concern. "Who did this? Why would somebody lock you in the shed?"

"I don't know." She bit her lower lip as tears threatened once again. "I didn't see who did it. I didn't see anyone around and I don't know why anyone would want to do such a thing."

"You need to call Dillon." Adam sat on the sofa next to her. "There's no way this was some kind of a freak accident. Somebody had to close the door and fasten the padlock."

A new chill raced through her. Yes, she needed to call Dillon. She had no idea what intention the person had when they'd locked her in the shed, but there was no way it was good.

Dillon pulled up in front of his ranch house. It was the place he'd once thought would be filled with love and the sound of children laughing. He'd never dreamed he'd come home each night to a dark and lonely place.

He killed his headlights and got out of the car. He'd eaten a burger at the café and now hoped he could empty his mind enough to get a good night's sleep. His brain had worked overtime all day. As if the murder investigation wasn't enough, the kiss he'd shared with Cassie had intruded into his thoughts throughout the entire day.

He unlocked his front door and walked in. Minutes later he was in his recliner with a beer in hand. When he'd bought this three-bedroom, two-bath house set on ten acres of land, he'd never dreamed he'd be living here alone.

He'd made so many plans with Stacy, the girl he'd fallen in love with when they'd both been high school juniors, and he'd been utterly blindsided when she'd not only left him, but had also left Bitterroot for life in a big city. He'd heard through the grapevine that she'd moved to Chicago. He hoped she'd found whatever she'd been looking for.

Sipping his beer, he tried to remember kissing Stacy. Strange, he couldn't remember what it felt like. Instead thoughts of kissing Cassie filled his head.

Her lips had been so hot and so wonderfully inviting. Damn the woman. He needed to keep his distance from her. He was convinced she was just another Stacy waiting to happen and he couldn't go through that kind of thing again. He'd rather be alone than take a chance with her.

He finished his beer and got up from the chair. Now all he wanted was to shower off the Oklahoma dust and then hit the hay. He'd just entered the master bath when his phone rang.

"Chief, sorry to bother you," Brenda Kline, the night dispatcher said.

"No problem, what's up?"

"I just got a call from Adam Benson out at the Holiday ranch. He said something about Cassie being locked up in a shed and they need you out there."

"On my way," he replied. His stomach tightened as he left the house and got into his car.

Cassie locked in a shed? Had she been hurt? What in the hell was going on now? Had it just been some sort of freak accident? If that was the case then why would they call him?

He wished he'd gotten more information. It was a fifteen-minute drive from his home to the Holiday ranch. He made it in twelve.

Adam greeted him at the back door. "She's in the great room," he said.

She was huddled in the corner of the sofa with the same purple throw wrapped around her shoulders. Her eyes appeared positively haunted as she greeted him.

"What happened?" he asked, fighting the impulse to grab her up and pull her to his chest. She looked so small and so frightened, but he was grateful to see that she appeared physically unharmed.

"I decided to go into the shed to grab some things and while I was inside somebody shut and locked the door behind me." Her face paled and she pulled the throw more tightly around her.

"I heard her screaming and unlocked the shed," Adam said.

"What were you doing outside at this time of night?" Dillon stared at the ranch foreman.

"I walk around every night to make sure all the gates are locked and everything is buttoned down," he replied. "I'm just grateful I heard her screaming, otherwise she might have been in there all night or…" His voice trailed off.

Dillon frowned. "Do you think this was some kind of a joke? Maybe one of the other men thought it would be funny?"

"No way," Adam replied flatly. "There's nothing funny about this and none of my men would have done anything to frighten Cassie."

"Before you heard her and unlocked the door did you see anyone else around?" Dillon asked.

Adam shook his head. "No, nobody."

"How did you happen to have a key to the shed?" Dillon was still struggling to figure out the how and why of what had happened.

"As the foreman, I have keys to all the ranch out-buildings." Adam pulled a key ring out of his pocket with dozens of keys.

"Dillon, Adam isn't the bad guy here," Cassie said softly. "He's the one who let me out, not the one who locked me in."

"Maybe one of the men from the ranch next door is responsible," Adam said, his disgust obvious in his voice. "We all know Raymond Humes's men love to cause trouble. One of those creeps was probably skulking around and thought this would be a funny thing to do. It sounds like their sick sense of humor."

Dillon had to admit that it did sound like something one of those men would do. Still, he had a bad feeling in the pit of his gut. "I'll take it from here," he told Adam. "Could you gather up all the men in the dining room?"

"Of course." Adam gazed at Cassie, a frown etched across his forehead. "Are you sure you're okay?" he asked her.

"I'm fine. Thank you, Adam."

"I'm just glad I was at the right place at the right time. I'll see you in the morning." With a nod at Dillon, Adam went out the back door.

"Are you sure you're okay?" Dillon asked. He eased down on the sofa next to her. "You weren't hurt?"

"I'm not hurt, but I'm not really okay. I keep wondering what would have happened if Adam hadn't shown up when he did." She pulled the throw more tightly around her.

Stay professional, Dillon told himself. Don't let your emotions get involved. Still, it was damned difficult to stay emotionally removed from her when her eyes seemed to need some sort of reassurance and she leaned toward him as if desperate for his arms around her.

He couldn't offer her reassurance until he got to the bottom of things, and he refused to embrace her because he feared he'd never want to let her go.

He got up off the sofa and shoved his hands in his

pockets. "I need to go check out that shed and talk to your men. Which shed was it?" He knew there were several on the property.

"It's the smaller one closest to the house."

"Will you be all right here alone?" She didn't look as if she would ever be all right again.

She roused herself from the sofa, clutching the throw around her shoulders. "I'll be okay as long as I lock the door behind you."

They reached the door and he turned to face her. "This shouldn't take too long and I'll come back in when I'm finished."

She nodded, her eyes still simmering pools of fear. "You know what I thought when I was in that shed?" She released a small, shaky laugh that had nothing to do with humor. "For just a brief moment I thought the door was going to swing open and somebody was going to attack me with an ax."

Dillon's heart squeezed tight. "There's no reason to believe this has anything to do with Sam's murder or the others."

"Logically I know that. I just don't understand why somebody would do that to me."

"I'm hoping I can find the answer. I'll see you in a little while." He left the house before he could give in to his desire to hold her tightly against him.

He stopped by his car and retrieved gloves and a couple of evidence bags. If nothing else he intended to take the padlock and see if he could lift any prints off it besides Adam's and Cassie's.

He clicked on his flashlight and headed to the shed. The door remained open and a look inside showed a couple stacks of boxes.

Why would somebody lock Cassie inside the small structure? Was the motive innocent? Somebody who thought it would be funny? Or was the motive much more insidious? He thought of Cassie's last words and his stomach clenched. Still, there was no way he could tie this incident into Sam Kelly's murder.

He pulled on his gloves and took off the padlock and dropped it into the evidence bag. The odds were minimal that he would be able to pull out a usable print, but at least he'd try.

He returned to his car, put the bag into his truck and then headed for the dining room at the back of the cowboy motel. Maybe one of the men would confess that they'd locked her in as a joke. Right, and maybe he'd grow a blond beard tomorrow, he thought drily.

Adam had gathered all the men, and as Dillon entered the dining room he did a quick head count. "Where's Brody?" he asked. The big, brooding cowboy was the only one missing from the group.

"He left about an hour ago," Sawyer said.

"We think he has a secret girlfriend. He's been leaving in the evenings a couple times a week," Mac McBride added.

Dillon made a mental note to talk to Brody the next day. "I'm assuming Adam has already told you all what happened. Anyone want to 'fess up?" Dillon asked.

"None of us would ever do anything to scare or hurt Cassie," Sawyer said, and the rest of the men echoed that sentiment loud and clear.

"It was probably one of those weasels from Humes's ranch," Flint McCay said angrily. "This stunt has their fingerprints all over it."

"Yeah, they're probably over there laughing their asses off right now," Sawyer said angrily.

Dillon raised his hands to quiet them all. "As soon as I leave here I'll be heading over there to question them. In the meantime I want you all to call me if you see somebody here on the property who doesn't belong."

Knowing he wouldn't get any answers to explain the mystery, Dillon left and headed back to the house. Cassie stood by the back door waiting for him.

She unlocked the door and let him inside. She looked as if she'd pulled herself together in the short time that he'd been gone. She no longer had the blanket around her shoulders, and the simmering fear that had been in her eyes was gone.

"I'm sure none of my men locked me in the shed," she said with a slight upward thrust of her chin.

"I'm not sure about anything," he replied.

"Did any of them confess?"

"No, but I didn't expect them to. I took the padlock off the door and I'm going to dust it for prints, but I'm not optimistic about getting anything useful from it. I'm also going to head over to the Humes place now and ask some questions there."

Her chin dropped and her lower lip trembled slightly.

He couldn't help himself. He reached out and grabbed her hand with his. Hers felt tiny and cold. He squeezed it gently. "It's going to be all right, Cassie."

She nodded. "I'm sure this was just somebody's idea of a stupid joke. Or maybe Raymond Humes has told his men to endlessly torment me since he can't wait for me to decide to sell the ranch to him."

He dropped her hand. "I'll let you know if I learn anything. Why don't you take my private cell phone number." He waited while she got her cell phone and they exchanged contact information. "Okay, then I'll just be off. In the meantime, watch your back, Cassie."

He didn't feel good about leaving her, but took some comfort in the fact that whoever had locked her in the shed hadn't physically attacked her. She'd been out there all alone in the dark, an easy prey for somebody waiting in the darkness. Thank God she'd only been locked inside and not hurt.

It was almost midnight by the time he got home. Talking to Humes's ranch hands had yielded nothing except the reminder that most of those men were lowlifes. They had all alibied each other even as they laughed about Cassie getting locked into her own shed.

He now undressed and got into bed. His body was

weary but his mind raced. He hoped it had all been a tasteless joke. He desperately wanted to believe that this wasn't the beginning of a reign of terror.

Chapter 5

"I'm so glad you're here," Cassie said to Nicolette Taylor the next morning. Her friend had stopped by for coffee and the two women now sat at the kitchen table. "I'm in desperate need of a little girl talk."

Nicolette's dark eyes radiated sympathy. "I wanted to call you the minute I heard about Sam's murder, but I figured you'd be busy with Dillon and the investigation. Does he have any idea who is responsible?"

"If he does, he's not telling me," Cassie replied. She wanted to confide to Nicolette that she and Dillon had kissed, that the kiss had rocked her to her very core, but she decided to keep it to herself for now. After all, it might never happen again and she doubted it had meant anything to him. "He was out here again last night because somebody locked me in my shed."

"What?" Nicolette looked at her in shock.

Cassie told her about what had transpired the night before and in the telling a new chill swept through her. "Anyway, all's well that ends well, right?" She forced a lightness into her tone.

Nicolette frowned. "Do you have any idea who did it?"

"None, but if I was speculating I'd say Raymond Humes and his men were behind it. He's so desperate for me to sell to him I think he'd do almost anything."

"Are you going to sell to him?"

Cassie sighed and wrapped her fingers around her coffee cup. "I feel like I have one foot here and one foot back in New York City. I know Raymond would be the last man Aunt Cass would want me to sell to, but I also know he'd pay me enough that I could reopen a shop and not have to worry about finances for a long time."

"And what about all your men?"

Cassie's heart squeezed. "I don't want them to be displaced, but I also tell myself they're all grown men and hard workers and they wouldn't have problems finding positions on other ranches in the area."

"You know your aunt Cass loved this ranch, but she would also want you to be happy," Nicolette replied. "I want you to be happy, Cassie, no matter what you choose to do."

"Right now I think my happiness isn't here, and Raymond's offer is looking darned good."

A knock on the back door interrupted their conversation. "It's open," Cassie called. Brody Booth walked in.

"Sorry to bother you but Adam wanted me to come and tell you that some of the fencing is down in the west pasture and he and a couple of men will be working there for most of the morning," he said.

"Why is the fencing down?" she asked.

Brody's eyes flashed. "Looks like it was pulled down by somebody during the night. Cattle got out but we've managed to round up all of them. He wasn't sure if you wanted to call Chief Bowie and make a report."

Cassie frowned thoughtfully. "No, we won't make a report this time. Dillon has enough on his mind right now without us piling more on him." Even saying his name pulled a blush of heat to her face.

"Okay, I'll tell Adam."

"Thanks, Brody," Cassie replied.

When the big cowboy left the kitchen she turned back to Nicolette to see one of her friend's dark brows raised in open speculation. "You say Dillon's name with the same longing that I say Lucas's name."

"Don't be ridiculous," Cassie scoffed and then released a deep sigh. "Okay, maybe I'm feeling a certain way about him," she admitted.

"And does he feel a certain way about you?" Nicolette asked.

"He kissed me and then he told me it was a big mistake," Cassie confessed.

Nicolette sat up straighter in her chair. "Hold up, Dillon kissed you? When and where? I want all the details, girlfriend."

Cassie nodded and told her about the evening Dillon had come in for dinner and the night ending with him kissing her.

"So how do you really feel about him?" Nicolette asked.

"Confused." Cassie paused to take a drink of her coffee. She set the cup down and cast her gaze out the window. "I don't want to make a mistake, Nicolette. I've already lived up to all my parents' expectations that I'd be a loser."

"Oh, Cassie, that's so not true," Nicolette protested.

"But it is true."

Nicolette frowned. "Cassie, at some point you're going to have to accept that your parents mentally and emotionally abused you and no matter what you do or become in your life it won't be good enough for them."

"I let them down. They had big plans for me. I didn't finish college and my big dream of a successful shop selling my artwork was a bust…"

"Cassie, you closed the shop to come out here when you got this inheritance. The shop wasn't a failure."

Cassie cast Nicolette a wry look. "Nicolette, be honest. We both know we couldn't have hung on much longer with the shop. And now I don't know whether to keep this place or sell out, and until I make up my mind about that I hate to pursue a relationship with anyone."

"It's hard to ignore chemistry." Nicolette said with a small smile. "And Dillon is a great guy." She gazed at her wristwatch. "Speaking of great guys, I need to get back home to mine." She picked up her cup and carried it to the sink.

Together they walked to the back door. "Thanks for stopping by," Cassie said.

"You know if you ever get scared staying here by yourself, you'd always be welcomed to stay with us."

"Thanks, I appreciate that, but I'm fine. Besides, I've got a bunch of big, burly cowboys to protect me."

Nicolette pulled her into a quick hug. "I just want you to be happy, Cassie."

"I'm working on it."

Happiness. It had been fleeting in Cassie's life so far, she thought as she returned to the table after Nicolette left. Her childhood had been a frantic desire of trying to please her parents. There certainly hadn't been much happiness there. Any further thoughts she might have on the subject was interrupted when Dillon knocked on the back door.

She couldn't help the way her heart caught in her throat when he walked inside. She scrambled up from the table. "Morning, Dillon. There's coffee if you want a cup."

"I believe I'll take you up on that," he replied.

As he sat at the table she grabbed a cup and filled it and then returned to the chair. "How are you doing after last night's scare?" he asked.

"I'm okay. Did you find out anything when you spoke to Humes's men?"

"Nothing."

She gave him a small smile. "Why am I not surprised? We had some fencing torn down sometime during the night and guess who I think is guilty?"

His thick-lashed gray eyes darkened. "Why didn't you call me to report it?"

"I figured you had enough on your plate without dealing with nuisance nonsense," she replied.

"Cassie, you need to let me know about everything that's going on."

She loved the way her name sounded falling from his lips. She loved the way he looked seated at her kitchen table. He was so tall, so masculine, and it was as if he owned all the air in the room. She stared down into her coffee cup.

There was definitely some kind of weird chemistry going on between them as far as she was concerned. Not that she intended to do anything about it.

He was here to talk crime with her. If Sam hadn't been murdered and those skeletons hadn't been found, the odds were that she wouldn't have exchanged more than friendly pleasantries with the handsome chief of police for as long as she was a resident in this town.

"Cassie?"

She looked up at him.

"Are you sure you're all right?"

"Positive. I'm just a little tired. I had a hard time falling asleep last night. I'm planning on heading to bed early this evening to catch up. I'll bet you could use an early night, too."

He crooked up a dark brow. She widened her eyes. "Not that I meant that as an invitation…"

He grinned, that gorgeous smile that made her think of cool nights and warm bodies and their very hot kiss. "I'm just teasing you a little bit. God knows we could both use a few laughs right about now."

"You're right. I feel like there hasn't been much to laugh about around here for a very long time."

He took a drink from his cup. "I haven't forgotten that I owe you a meal. How about I pick you up later tonight and we go to the café for a bite to eat? I promise I'll have you back here early enough that you can still get a good night's sleep."

Cassie's heart beat a quickened rhythm. Had he just asked her for a date or had she somehow misheard?

"I know it's spur of the moment. Maybe you already have other plans," he continued.

"No, not at all. Sure, I'd love to go to dinner," she replied.

"How's six o'clock?"

"Perfect."

"And now I'd better get to work." He rose from the table. "I'll see you this evening at six. Bring your appetite."

She remained seated at the table as he walked out

the back door. The man was confusing the heck out of her. Kissing her had been a mistake and yet apparently inviting her out to dinner was okay.

It hadn't even entered her mind to turn down his invitation. What was he doing? What on earth was she doing? Nicolette's words fluttered through her mind. *It's hard to ignore chemistry.* And there was definitely some strange, wonderful chemistry at work between her and Dillon.

Her heart was definitely torn, but her head was already going through the clothes in her closet trying to decide what to wear this evening.

Bitch.

He'd seen her just a few minutes ago leave the house in her tight blue dress and whore high heels, running to get into Dillon Bowie's pickup truck.

He also knew she'd talked to her friend about selling the ranch to Raymond Humes. She was nothing but an ungrateful whore, and whores deserved to die.

If she thought it had been scary to be locked in the shed, Cassie Peterson had no idea what terror was about to rain down on her head.

She was no better than his slutty mother who had taken him with her when she slept with half the town while his father worked the night shift.

He fisted his hands as he remembered those nights when he'd stood outside a motel room all alone in the dark while his mother got busy with one of her lovers.

A smile curved his lips as he remembered the

satisfaction of strangling her to death. He'd only been fourteen years old, but he'd known what had to be done. He'd driven her car to a wooded area and had buried her body there. He'd then driven back to one of the seedy motels she frequented and left the car there.

Oh, yes, he knew how to deal with whores, and he knew what had to be done with Cassie.

Cassie's scent filled the interior of his truck as Dillon drove toward town for dinner at the Bitter-root Café. A million times over the course of the day he'd thought about canceling on her. But here he was, enjoying the play of sunset in her hair and the sight of her shapely legs beneath the short, royal blue dress she wore.

"It's a beautiful night," she said.

"Yes, it is," he agreed. He just hoped he didn't get any calls that might take him away from a meal with her.

He had a feeling the only person who might be in danger tonight was him. Cassie looked totally hot and the memory of kissing her was forefront in his mind. Definitely dangerous considering his heart had been closed for so long and she was probably the last woman he should be drawn to. And yet drawn he was.

"Are you hungry?" he asked.

"Starving. I skipped lunch and I'm looking forward to a meal I didn't have to cook…especially since my cooking skills are fairly nonexistent," she said. He felt her gaze lingering on him. "I'd love to paint you sometime. You have a beautiful, masculine face with so much character."

"Thanks," he said as his cheeks grew warm. "You know your face isn't too hard to look at, either."

"Was that a compliment, Chief Bowie?" she returned lightly.

"I believe it was," he agreed. He wasn't sure exactly what he wanted from her. He wasn't at all clear what he was doing with her, but the only thing that was certain was he didn't want to stop.

She was not only gorgeous, but she was also intelligent and feisty. She spoke exactly what was on her mind and he liked that about her. He just wanted to get to know her a little bit better. Surely there was no harm in that.

He pulled up in front of the Bitterroot Café, where the parking lot was full, as it was on most evenings. The brash redheaded owner Daisy Martin greeted them as they walked in the door.

"I've got a booth with your name on it unless you want to wait for a table," she said.

"A booth is just fine," Dillon said, and Cassie nodded in agreement.

As Daisy led them to an empty yellow vinyl booth, several people greeted them both. Once they were seated and waiting for a waitress Dillon smiled at her. "You know by tomorrow we'll be the talk of the town."

She returned his smile and picked up the menu. "Living on the Holiday ranch I'm used to being gossiped about. But I've never heard any gossip about you so this is going to be a first."

"Oh, not a first," he protested. "Several years ago there was enough gossip going on about me to last a lifetime, but that's a story for another time."

She cast him a curious gaze and then looked down at her menu. He hadn't meant to be cryptic, but talking about Stacy's blindside of him wasn't something he wanted to do in public over a casual dinner.

Julia Hatfield appeared at their table with glasses of ice water and her order pad. "Cassie, nice to see you," she said. "And, Chief Bowie, it's always a pleasure to see you. Now, what can I get you both?"

"I'd like the chicken fried steak with mashed potatoes," Cassie said and closed her menu.

"Pot roast for me." Dillon didn't have to study the menu since he ate here practically every night.

"What about to drink?" Julia asked. Cassie ordered a sweet tea and Dillon ordered a soda. "I just want to let you know you might want to save room for dessert. Daisy made a flourless chocolate cake with raspberry drizzle and it's getting rave reviews."

"Hmm, sounds good," Cassie agreed.

"I'm still a loyal fan of Daisy's apple pie," he replied.

"She does make a mean apple pie," Julia agreed.

"I'd rather have apple pie for dessert than anything else," Dillon said.

Julia smiled. "I'll see that you get an extra big

piece tonight." She took their menus and then left the booth.

Dillon leaned back and studied the woman across from him. Cassie Peterson wasn't classically beautiful, but with her short, curly blond hair and sparkling blue eyes she was cute as a bug. Her nose was slightly upturned and her lips were perfect cupid bows.

"You do know you're staring at me," she said.

"Sorry, I was just thinking it's nice to see a smile on your face. Too often in the past I've seen you upset."

"The same goes for you. I usually see you looking all stern and businesslike. But I don't want to talk about anything negative this evening. I just want to enjoy a nice meal in good company."

"Amen," he replied.

Their drinks arrived, followed quickly by their meals. As they ate they talked about a variety of topics. She loved old rock-and-roll music and he preferred country. She enjoyed movies that were comedies and he liked action flicks.

They argued good-naturedly about the merits of owning a dog versus having a cat, about hot chocolate or hot cider in the winter, and by that time they were finished with the meal and had received their desserts and coffee.

"Hmm, this is yummy," she said after taking a bite of her chocolate cake. "And this has been so nice. Thank you for inviting me, Dillon."

"It has been nice," he agreed. "You're easy to be with, Cassie."

"What did you expect?"

"I don't know, maybe that you'd be angry with me for believing one of your men is guilty."

She smiled, the gesture lightening her eyes, making him want to fall into the beautiful depths. "We can agree to disagree on that issue and many others. That doesn't mean I'm going to be bitchy with you."

"Are you ever bitchy?" he asked humorously.

She laughed. "Definitely when I first wake up. I'm not much of a morning person until I've had my coffee."

"I'll have to remember that." Now why had he said that? As if he anticipated spending an early morning with her.

He gazed toward the door and his stomach tightened as he saw Lloyd Green, Zeke Osmond and Ace Sanders walk in. They were all Humes's men.

"Brace yourself, here comes trouble," he said softly to Cassie just before the men reached their booth.

"Well, well, don't you two look all cozy," Lloyd said as he hooked his thumbs in his belt loops and rocked back on his heels. Behind him Zeke and Ace snickered.

"Evening, boys," Dillon said evenly.

"Don't you look lovely, Cassie," Lloyd said and then looked back at Dillon. "I've got to say, I'm surprised to see you here with her."

"Why would you be surprised?" Dillon asked.

"I didn't know you still had a nose for that city stuff," Lloyd replied. "I'd a thought you learned your lesson with Stacy."

Every muscle in Dillon's body tensed. "And I'd a thought you'd be smart enough not to bait the man who is investigating you and your friends for all kinds of crimes," he replied.

"And I'm not stuff, thank you very much," Cassie replied with obvious irritation.

"You're hot stuff," Zeke said with a leering grin.

"You got that right," Ace added and jabbed Zeke in the side with a snicker.

"Lloyd, take your friends and get in a booth or get out," Daisy's voice rang out as she approached them. "Sorry, Chief," she said as the three men headed to a booth in the back.

"No problem, Daisy," he replied.

"Too bad you can't arrest stupid," she exclaimed as she shook her head and then returned to the counter by the front door.

"I can't believe that a town that produced so many wonderful people also produced them," Cassie said drily.

"I imagine every town has their share of bullies and troublemakers." Dillon willed himself to relax, but he couldn't get back the peaceful enjoyment he'd felt before Humes's men had shown up and intruded.

Minutes later they were in his truck, his headlights piercing through the darkness as they headed back to her place. "I'm so full I should sleep like a baby tonight," she said.

"Me, too. I could have done without the apple pie but I always like a little sweet at the end of a meal."

What he'd really like would be to end the night with the sweetness of her lips on his. He'd been thinking about kissing her again throughout most of the evening.

As they got closer to her place and she talked about some of the people who had been in the café, his stomach tightened with the desire to hold her in his arms.

Don't be a fool, a little voice whispered inside his head. *Just don't go there with her.* The last thing he wanted was to make her believe he wanted a relationship with her when he didn't. There was no reason to lead her on.

Once they reached the ranch he parked by the back door and she got her keys out of her purse. "Thank you again, Dillon," she said as they reached the door. "I've really enjoyed the evening."

The moonlight loved her features and his heart quickened its pace. He didn't plan it, but before he knew it she was in his arms. As she raised her face he captured her lips with his.

She tasted of dark chocolate, sweet raspberry and white-hot desire. Her body was invitingly warm against his when he pulled her closer.

She curled into him as if wanting to be as close as possible. He stroked a hand through her springy soft hair and deepened the kiss.

He finally tore his mouth from hers and peered

down at her. "Was that just another mistake?" she asked as she raised a finger to her lower lip.

"Probably," he replied. "I've got to tell you, Cassie, there's something about you that makes me want more, but I'm not looking for love right now in my life."

She tilted her head slightly, her gaze curious. "I'm not sure that's what I'm looking for, either. But then what are we doing?"

"I don't know," he confessed. "All I do know is I like spending time with you."

"And I like spending time with you," she replied. "And I definitely like kissing you." Her eyes shimmered in the moonlight as her words heated his blood once again.

He dropped his arms to his sides and stepped back from her. "I think we've done enough kissing for one night. I'll talk to you tomorrow."

"Good night, Dillon, and thanks again."

"'Night, Cassie."

He waited until she'd unlocked her door and was safely inside and then he walked back to his truck and headed home, his thoughts working overtime.

Was what he felt for Cassie strictly sexual? It was possible. It had certainly been a long time since he'd been with any woman. As chief of police he'd been wary of dating a woman from Bitterroot, knowing that his relationships would be scrutinized by the entire town. The last thing he'd wanted to do was tarnish his reputation by dating a series of women as he tried to find that special one.

Still, he liked Cassie's company. He enjoyed the sound of her laughter. Having left her only moments before, he already anticipated the time when he would see her again.

He knew it was possible she'd eventually be lured back to the big city, so the one thing he absolutely would not do was give his heart to Cassie Peterson.

Chapter 6

Cassie practically danced into her house, her lips still holding the very hot imprint of his, and her body warmed by his embrace. The evening had been wonderful. Dillon had been more than wonderful. Everything she had learned about him had only made her want to know more.

She headed up the stairs, her mind playing and replaying every minute of their time together. She'd always had the impression that he was stern and more than a bit unyielding, but tonight she'd discovered he had a terrific personality with a sense of humor that only increased her attraction to him.

When she reached her bedroom she stripped off her clothes and got into a short pink nightgown and then padded into the adjoining bathroom to take off her makeup.

During their dinner conversation Dillon had laughed often and his eyes had held a lightness she'd never seen there before. Definitely sexy, she thought.

Minutes later she was in bed with an artist pad, a charcoal pencil in hand and Dillon's handsome features burned into her brain.

For the next half an hour she worked on the sketch, not stopping until she was satisfied she'd captured each and every bold line of his face. When she was finished she stared at the sketch. She'd managed to capture his strong jawline and his straight nose perfectly. Lines fanned out from the outer corners of his eyes, giving him character.

She wasn't sure she'd gotten his mouth just right. She'd worked on it for a long time in an attempt to capture the sensual curl of his smile, but it still needed a little more work.

Tomorrow, she thought as she set the sketch on her nightstand and then got up and went into the bathroom once again, this time to wash her hands.

By the time she returned to bed it was a little after ten o'clock. She turned off the lamp on the nightstand and then cuddled down beneath the covers.

Dillon. She'd half wanted to grab him by the hand and bring him up to this bed. No man had ever stirred such a well of longing inside her before. She had no idea where their relationship was going. She wasn't sure if it was smart to allow it to go anywhere. If she decided to sell the ranch and leave Bitterroot there was no way she would expect him to pull up roots and go with her. And a long-distance relationship would be ridiculous to try to maintain. Besides, he'd told her he wasn't looking for love in his life.

Still, with all these negatives playing in her mind, she couldn't imagine not exploring whatever crazy emotions they were experiencing with each other.

She thought of what Lloyd had said in the café. Who in the heck was Stacy? The question lingered in her mind as she drifted off to sleep.

She awoke with a jolt, her heart racing so fast she could scarcely catch her breath. She sat up and shot a glance at her clock. The illuminated numbers indicated it was just after one.

What had awakened her? She didn't remember having any kind of a dream. She held her breath and listened…and heard the faint pad of footsteps coming from downstairs.

Her heart squeezed so tightly she couldn't breathe. Somebody was inside the house! How had they gotten in? Oh, God, who was down there and what did they want?

"Cassie." The hoarse, sibilant whisper drifted up the stairs and raised goose bumps on her arms. A loud bang resounded, shaking the walls.

Cassie stifled a scream. Oh, God, what was happening? The back of her throat closed up as she grabbed her cell phone, slid from the bed and frantically looked around. What should she do? Where

could she hide? She definitely didn't want to con-
front whoever was inside.

The overstuffed closet. She quickly ducked inside and closed the closet doors. Another loud crash
sounded. She whimpered and tried to burrow deeper
behind the hanging clothing. What was going on?
Who was in her house?

With shaking fingers she dialed Dillon's number, nearly sobbing when he answered on the first
ring. "Somebody's in the house," she whispered into
the phone.

"Where are you?" His voice held urgency.

"I'm in the closet in my bedroom. Hurry, Dillon,
I think he's coming up the stairs."

"I'm on my way."

She clicked off the phone, afraid that if Dillon
said anything more the person coming up the stairs
might hear his voice and know she was hiding in
the closet.

"Cassie." The guttural voice was closer...so horrifyingly close. *Don't open the closet door. Please,
don't open the closet door.* Once again something
slammed into the wall and this time the crackling
of Sheetrock filled the air. All the muscles in her
body jumped in fear.

Who was it and what was he doing? Oh, God,
it sounded like he was destroying the entire house.
What did he want from her? And what was he going
to do to her when he opened the closet door and
found her? And there was no doubt in her mind he
would find her.

She shoved her fist into her mouth to staunch her need to release a scream of utter terror. Tears washed down her face as she waited in the dark closet... anticipating something horrible happening.

She squeezed her eyes tightly closed, like a child who believed if the bogeyman wasn't seen, then he didn't exist. But he did exist and he was coming closer... He might be here in the room with her at this very moment.

The faint sound of a siren drifted to her.

Dillon! Oh, God, hurry...hurry!

The only sound she now heard was her own breathing. Rapid and frantic she gulped in air as her tears raced faster and faster down her cheeks. Did the silence mean the person was gone?

Or was it a ruse and he was just waiting for her to step out of the closet? She remained curled up in the darkness for several long, terrifying, silent minutes.

"Cassie? Cassie, are you in here?"

The deep, familiar voice shuddered relief through her. "In here. Dillon, I'm in here," she called. The closet doors slid open and she began to cry in deep, wrenching sobs.

He reached behind all the hanging clothes and pulled her up and out. She plastered herself against him, only then allowing her terror to release in earnest. She buried her face into the crook of his neck, finding comfort in his familiar scent, in the strength of his arms surrounding her.

"It's okay, Cassie. You're safe now," he murmured

softly as one of his hands slowly stroked up and down her back.

Safe…thank goodness she was safe. She drew in several deep breaths in an attempt to steady herself. It was only as she stepped away from him that she saw how dark and turbulent his eyes were.

He led her to the bed and then pulled out his cell phone. "I'm just going to call and get Michael and Juan out here." As he made the quick call she shivered and fought back a new burst of tears. Who had been in her house? Who had broken in in the middle of the night and what had they wanted from her?

"Now, tell me exactly what happened," he said when he was off the phone. He sat next to her and took one of her hands in his.

"I was asleep and something woke me up." She told him about the whisper of her name and then the loud noises she'd heard.

"You didn't recognize the voice?" he asked.

She shook her head. "No, I just know it was husky and creepy." She shivered. "How did he get inside the house?"

He gently squeezed her hand. "The window next to the back door was broken. Apparently, he broke it to reach in and unlock the door." He released her hand and stood. "I'd like you to come downstairs and wait there until after my men are done in here."

"Okay, just let me grab my robe." She wanted it not only to cover her for modesty's sake because the officers would be here soon but also because she was icy cold and felt as if she would never be warm

ing out in the moonlight with an ax in his hand, but it would have been nice if Juan and Michael had come back with something.

He put Juan to work photographing and measuring the gashes in the walls as Michael tried to pull prints off the broken window and back door.

Dillon had little hope that the men would be able to collect anything worthwhile. He was relatively certain that whoever had broken in had been smart enough to wear gloves.

The bastard was so smart he hadn't been caught for over fifteen years. Dillon knew in his gut this was an evil that had been dormant for all these years and something had awakened it once again.

He supposed it might be possible that it was a copycat, but he didn't think so. His belief that this was the same person who had killed those seven teenage boys was nothing more than a strong gut instinct, but it was a feeling he couldn't deny or ignore.

He left Cassie on the sofa and went into the kitchen to check Michael's progress. "I've got nothing," he said at Dillon's appearance. "I can't even lift a partial. If I was to guess, when he opened the door he wiped the knob clean."

"Let's do a walk-through and see if we find anything else he might have unintentionally left behind," Dillon said.

It was almost three thirty when Dillon said a frustrated goodbye to his men. Cassie sat at the kitchen table with a hot cup of tea before her and he joined her there.

"You aren't going to leave, are you?" she asked, a faint desperation in her voice.

He hadn't thought about what might happen for the rest of the night, but seeing the festering fear that still lingered in her eyes, knowing the fear for her that lingered in his heart, he knew he couldn't leave her for the remainder of the night here all alone.

"I'm not going anywhere," he assured her. "I'm staying for the rest of the night. You go on up to bed and I'll stay down here on the sofa. I'll see to it that nothing happens to you."

She curled her fingers around her teacup. "Could we just stay up and talk for a little while longer? I'm not quite ready to go back upstairs just yet."

"We need to talk about what has to happen tomorrow," he replied. "To start with you need to get an alarm installed here."

"Actually, I already have one. I just haven't used it for a while. But can we talk about that kind of stuff in the morning? Right now what I really need is just some small talk to take my mind off what happened." She offered him a weak smile. "A girl has to have some time to process when a man tries to kill her with an ax."

His gut twisted in knots. Thank God he'd gotten here as fast as he had. He didn't even want to think about how terrible the night might have ended if he hadn't arrived when he had.

"Why don't we go sit in the great room?" She finished the last of her tea and carried her cup to the sink. Together they left the kitchen and sat on either ends of the sofa.

"Why don't you tell me about Stacy."

He looked at her in surprise, and then remembered that Lloyd Green had mentioned Stacy at the café earlier that evening. He hadn't talked about Stacy to anyone since she'd left town…since she'd left him.

"Stacy was my high school sweetheart and I thought she was the woman I would be spending the rest of my life with," he replied. "But it didn't work out that way."

"What happened?" She leaned slightly toward him, bringing to his nose her attractive scent.

"We dated and made plans together. My dream was to become chief of police here and once we married, Stacy would be a stay-at-home mother and we'd have a couple of children. After high school I got on the police force and she worked as a teacher's aide at the grade school. I bought the house where I live now and we moved in together and life was pretty good. At least I thought so at the time."

He shifted positions and continued, "On the day I was sworn in as chief of police, Stacy told me she wanted more out of life than what Bitterroot could offer and so she left."

He was grateful that his voice had been calm and steady and held none of the emotions that had gripped him at the time. He was surprised to realize that much of the pain of that time, of her abandonment, was finally gone.

"You didn't know she was unhappy?"

"I didn't have a clue. I thought everything was on track and assumed our next step was a wedding."

Cassie studied his features intently. "Did she break your heart?"

Stacy's leaving had utterly devastated him. She had shattered almost every dream he'd had for his life. "Maybe just a little," he confessed. "What about you? Any broken hearts in your past?" He not only was curious about her, but also wanted to get the topic of conversation off Stacy and his own failures.

"None," she replied after a moment of hesitation. "In the past I've always been too consumed about my work to have any deep, meaningful relationships."

"What about now? You and Adam seem pretty close."

She offered him the first real smile of the night. "Dillon, I wouldn't be kissing you like I have if Adam and I were like that."

Thinking of the kisses he'd shared with her instantly tightened his stomach muscles. "I think we should both get some sleep now," he said.

"You're right. It won't be that long and the sun will be shining." She got up from the sofa and he did the same. "I'll just get you a pillow and a blanket… unless you want to come upstairs and sleep in my bed."

There was a definite invitation in her eyes, an invitation he'd love to accept, but if they were going to go there then tonight definitely wasn't the right time.

"Cassie, that's really not a good idea. You've had a horrible scare and if and when we wind up in bed together, I want it to be on a night when we're both thinking clearly and nothing bad has happened."

She held his gaze for a long moment and then nodded. "Okay, I'll just grab you a pillow and a blanket."

Minutes later Dillon stretched out on the sofa, his mind going over all the events of the night. His gun was on the coffee table in easy reach and it was only now that the tight knot of fear that had been in the pit of his stomach since he'd heard Cassie's frightened voice on the phone slowly began to release.

Who had been in her house? Who had broken the window and then come inside with an ax and smashed up her walls? According to Juan the measurements and shape of the gashes in the Sheetrock were consistent with an ax or a hatchet. And why had that somebody come after Cassie?

She was okay for tonight, but what about tomorrow and the day after that…? In the morning he would insist she start using her alarm system every minute of every day, but that wasn't foolproof and he knew her men came and went into the house at will to speak to her about ranch business.

Her men.

It would have been so easy for one of them to break in, then when he heard the siren to run out and get back in his room and pretend to have been asleep when Juan and Michael had checked in with the men.

Dillon still believed there was a bad apple in the bunch, but that meant she also had men who would probably protect her with their lives. But who could she really trust? Who could he trust with her safety?

One thing was clear. She was the target of a killer and one way or another he would personally make sure she was safe until the person was no longer a threat.

He thought about her invitation to sleep in her bed, and a wave of heat washed over him. There was no question in his mind that if he'd gone upstairs with her they would have had sex. And there was no question that it would have been explosive and powerful.

But he'd wanted them both to be clearheaded if and when that happened. She had to understand that he had nothing emotionally to give her.

It would have been easy for him to take advantage of her tonight. She'd been frightened and needy and probably not thinking straight. If he was a different kind of man he would have taken her up on the offer, made love to her and not worried about her emotions.

He released a deep sigh and closed his eyes. Sometimes it sucked to be a good guy.

He'd almost gotten caught. He lay on his back and stared up at the dark ceiling. If he hadn't run out of the house when he had, Dillon would have seen him. He could only assume that she'd somehow managed to call for help.

Dammit, he'd wasted too much time whacking the walls and terrorizing Cassie when he should have just silently marched up the stairs and killed her while she slept.

And now she'd allowed Dillon to spend the night with her. She'd been his Madonna and now she was a whore. Rage pressed tightly against his ribs.

He no longer gave a damn that her death could possibly put the ranch up for sale, making the futures of all the men here uncertain.

If that happened he'd convince all the men to band together and buy the ranch. They could do it and that way Cass Holiday's legacy would continue on.

However, his need to see Cassie dead was much more personal than her potential betrayal of her aunt in a decision to sell the ranch to Raymond Humes.

Whores deserved to die. Next time he'd make sure he got the job done right. He'd screwed up tonight, but he was a patient man and was certain there would be a next time. He smiled to himself and closed his eyes.

Chapter 7

Cassie awoke to bright sunshine pouring through the sheer curtains in her bedroom window. She rolled over and looked at her clock and was shocked to see it was after nine. She hadn't slept this late since she'd moved here.

However, she'd never had somebody with an ax coming after her in the middle of the night before. Despite the lateness of the hour she stayed in bed several moments, thinking first about the terror of the night before and then about Dillon.

Thank God he'd arrived when he had. There was no question in her mind that he'd saved her life. But gratitude hadn't been what had driven her to invite him to her bed.

Yes, she knew his arms around her would have

comforted her and she knew any residual fear would have vanished as passion ruled. But that hadn't been the reason she'd wanted him in bed with her. It had been pure, unadulterated desire for him.

Surprisingly he hadn't hurt her feelings when he'd turned her down. She'd seen the sparks in his eyes and she'd heard longing in his voice even while he told her he'd bunk on the sofa.

If anything, by turning down her invitation he'd only made her like him more. She truly believed he'd had her best interests at heart. And maybe he was right; it had been a little bit of leftover fear that had made her want him immediately.

Was he still here or had he left to get back to his job as the chief of police in this town? She certainly couldn't expect him to stay with her forever when he was the town's head lawman.

Still, she jumped out of bed and pulled her robe around her, then went into the bathroom and brushed her teeth and hair. When she thought she was presentable enough she hurried down the stairs.

Dillon sat at the kitchen table, a cup of coffee before him. He greeted her with a pleasant smile. "Good morning."

"It will be a better morning after I get some coffee." She poured herself a cup and then joined him at the table.

"I hope you slept well," he said.

"I did," she admitted. "It took me a little while to fall asleep but when I did I was out like a light. What about you? You don't look any worse for the wear of spending the night on the sofa." In fact, he looked ridiculously handsome even though his shirt was slightly wrinkled and dark whiskers had appeared along his jaw.

"The sofa was very comfortable."

"I thought maybe you'd be gone by now. I realize you do have an important job in this town." She took a drink of her coffee.

"Right now I'm doing my job by being here," he replied. "I spoke to all of your men this morning and told them how important it was for them to keep an eye on you." He reached into his pocket and then placed a single key on the table.

"What's that?" she asked.

"I asked all the men who had keys to the house, and Adam told me he did. I took it from him. Right now I don't want anyone having keys to get inside."

"But the person who got in here last night didn't have a key. He broke the window."

Dillon nodded. "And I've already contacted Will Denver to come out and replace the windowpane sometime this afternoon. Is there anyone else that you know who has a key to the house?"

"No, just Adam." She took a sip of the coffee, leaned back in her chair and once again the taste of fear filled her mouth. "And I guess I'd better start setting the alarm system."

"Definitely, and if you don't mind, since I'm staying here I'd like to have the code." She told him the four-digit code. "Does anyone else know it?"

"No. I set it when I first had it installed and I never told anyone the code."

He nodded. "I know how your men come and go and my recommendation is that you don't let any of them inside the house when they are alone."

She stared at him and the fear that had momentarily filled her mouth spread throughout her entire body. "I thought everything would look brighter this morning but now I'm afraid all over again."

He leaned forward. "You need to be afraid, Cassie. Somebody broke in here last night with the intention of hurting you and right now we have no idea where the danger came from or where it might come from again." He frowned. "Is there somebody you can stay with for a while?"

"I'm not leaving here," she replied firmly. "This is my home. I have responsibilities here and I can't just take off and hide out. Besides, if somebody is after me, then I don't want to bring that danger to anyone else. We don't even know how long it will take before I'm not in danger anymore."

His frown deepened. "Then I think it's a good idea that I move in here for the time being."

Stunned surprise winged through her. "How are you going to do that? You have a full-time job and people in this town who depend on you to be there for them. You can't be here with me every day and night."

"You're right," he agreed. "I can't be here during the days, but I can be here in the evenings and overnight. I can make sure that what happened here last night doesn't happen again. I don't worry so much about the daytimes, especially since I put your men on notice to watch out for you, but it's the nights that concern me."

She pulled her robe more tightly around her. "I don't know what to say... Thank you seems ridiculously inadequate."

He offered her a small smile. "Cassie, this is what I do. I protect the people in this town with my life, and right now nobody is in more imminent danger than you."

Imminent danger. The very words scared her half to death. "Even with what happened last night I can't wrap my head around all of this," she replied.

It was as if they were talking about somebody else's life or the plot of a particularly scary horror movie. This couldn't really be happening to her and yet it was.

"So, what I'm really wondering is if you're ready for a roommate," he said.

"I'd be a fool to say no." She forced a smile to her lips but it only lasted a moment. "But the first thing I want to do this morning is get some of the men in here to fix the walls in the stairwell. I don't want that damage to be the first thing I see every morning when I come down the stairs." A shiver tried to work up her spine.

Yesterday morning she'd trusted all of her men without question, but she couldn't say the same thing this morning. She wasn't sure who she could trust anymore, except Dillon.

"Just make sure you don't have any of them in the house alone. If you want to ask several of them to come in and fix the wall, I'm comfortable with that. You do have some good men, Cassie. It's the potential bad one that worries me."

Was Sawyer, with his copper-colored eyes and easy smiles, really a killer? What about Mac McBride, who played his guitar and sang like an angel? And what about Adam, the man who had been her teacher and mentor since she'd arrived here? All the men's faces flashed through her head, only confusing her even more. If there was really a bad apple among the bunch, she couldn't begin to guess who it was.

"Cassie?"

Dillon's voice pulled her out of her dark thoughts. She flushed. "Sorry, I was deep in my own head thinking about which one of my men could be a killer."

"I just wanted to tell you that I need to go into the office and check in there and then I'll go to my house and pack a few things and be back here sometime later this afternoon." He gazed at her intently. "Will you be okay until I get back here?"

"I'll be fine," she assured him with another forced smile as he rose from the table. "I'll put on the alarm when you go out and once the men address the wall issue I won't open the door to anyone else but you."

What she really wanted to do was throw her arms around his waist and desperately cling to him. She wanted to beg him not to go and leave her here all alone. The terror she'd experienced last night was once again alive and kicking inside her, but she tried desperately to tamp it down.

She had to be stronger than her fear. If there was one thing life in Bitterroot had shown her it was that the people here were tough and resilient. Right now she needed to dig deep inside herself to find those very qualities. She got up and followed him to the door.

He reached out and cupped her chin with his hand. His gray eyes were still dark, but now held a caring that soothed her despite her situation.

"Lock yourself in, Cassie, and keep everyone else out." He dropped his hand back to his side. "I'll see you later." With that he left her alone.

She armed the alarm system and then went back upstairs for a quick shower and to dress for the day. So far the morning had held the same kind of surreal quality as the night before.

She couldn't believe he was actually going to move in here. For how long? Until he caught the killer? She'd been here six months and he hadn't caught the killer yet. How long would this danger exist for her? Until the madman met his goal and she was murdered?

Trying to release all her negative thoughts, she stepped beneath the warm shower spray and raised her face to the water. No matter how hard she tried to empty her brain, it refused to cooperate.

If she had been killed last night, who would have mourned her? Certainly not her parents, whom she hadn't heard from in the last five years. Nicolette would have been sad, but she had her own family and would have quickly gotten over any grief.

Cassie had lived her life completely alone and hadn't invited in people because she'd been so wrapped up in her need to be somebody.

Right now she was the somebody that some ax-wielding madman wanted to kill. With this thought, she quickly finished her shower and then pulled on a pair of jeans and a blouse and headed back downstairs.

The gashes on the wall were a grim reminder that she had to be careful. Somebody wanted her dead.

She stared out the great room window. Two men were on horseback and another pair was walking toward the stables. She was surrounded by people yet very alone in her ivory tower.

"Stop feeling sorry for yourself," she said aloud. Nobody liked a crybaby. She should get busy and get her mind off everything that was taking place.

She remembered Dillon being a fan of apple pie. She was fairly sure there was a recipe in one of the cookbooks that had belonged to her aunt Cass.

She'd bake a pie and get a couple of steaks out of the freezer. If Dillon was going to stay here to protect her then the least she could do in return was try to make sure he ate good meals. And maybe…just maybe she'd wind up in his arms again.

Dillon left Cassie's and went to his house first. He took a shower and then changed into a fresh uniform. He packed a large duffel bag, wondering how in the hell he was going to catch the person who had placed Cassie in his deadly sights.

He hoped that by spending more time at the ranch he'd get closer to the cowboys, and the guilty would somehow tip his hand. Was it possible Raymond Humes was really behind everything? Had the man paid somebody to terrorize Cassie in hopes she would sell the ranch to him?

Was one of Cassie's cowboys secretly working with Humes? That certainly didn't explain what had happened fifteen years ago with the dead boys in a grave beneath a shed.

He threw the last of his toiletries into the bag and then carried it out to his car and headed for the police station on Main Street.

Bitterroot was an anomaly among small-town America in that it was maintaining its existence, unlike so many other small communities that had died slow, painful deaths. Dillon took pride in that. He worked closely with the town council to ensure opportunities for the youth and did everything in his power to keep a pride of community alive.

"Hey, Chief," Annie greeted him as he walked through the police station door. "Brenda told me something bad happened out at the Holiday ranch overnight."

"Yeah, somebody went after Cassie with an ax," he replied.

Annie's eyes widened. "Since you're here I'm assuming she's okay."

"She's frightened, but okay."

"Did she see the person? Could she give you a description?" Annie asked.

"She didn't see him. He called out to her and she hid in her closet. She didn't recognize his voice, either." Dillon grimaced. "I wish she would have seen him so I could get him arrested."

"Do you think this has to do with the other murders that took place there?"

Dillon frowned. "I can't help but believe it's possible, but honest to God, Annie, I can't seem to get a handle on any of this."

"You will, Chief," Annie said with confidence. "Now, on another note, Leroy called this morning and wants you out at his place."

Dillon stifled a groan. "Another alien encounter?"

"I'm assuming. I tried to tell him I'd send out one of the other men but you know he'll only talk to you."

"I'll swing by there on my way back to the Holiday ranch this afternoon. Anything else earth-shattering I need to deal with?"

Annie smiled ruefully. "I'd say an ax murderer and invading aliens are more than enough."

"I'll be in the office until noon and then I'm taking off. I'm going to be staying out at Cassie's for the next week or so, but the fewer people who know that, the better."

Annie made a motion like she was zipping her lips. "Nobody will hear it from me."

"Thanks, Annie." He left the small lobby area

and peeked his head into the back room where the deputy desks were located. Nobody was working there at the moment.

The Bitterroot Police Department was small, consisting of fourteen deputies and one canine unit. There were four men on duty today and most of them spent their days out of the building.

Dillon went into his office and collapsed into his chair. He closed his eyes for several minutes and drew deep, even breaths in an attempt to find a new burst of energy.

If truth be told, while the sofa had been comfortable enough last night, sleep had been elusive. Each and every sound in the unfamiliar house had set him on edge. Twice he'd grabbed his gun, only to realize the sound he'd heard was the ice maker dropping ice in the refrigerator in the kitchen.

If that hadn't been enough to keep him awake, then knowing Cassie was just up a flight of stairs had tormented him more than just a little bit.

He swore he could smell the lilac scent of her throughout the long night even though logically he knew it was impossible. He'd even kicked himself more than once for not taking her up on her offer and spending the night in her bed.

He snapped his eyes open and got to work checking on the reports of activity that had occurred overnight in the town. Petty theft at the mercantile store, two speeding tickets given out on Main Street and a minor accident in the parking lot of the Watering Hole, the most popular bar in town.

Definitely nothing to rival an ax-swinging maniac chasing a vulnerable woman into the closet of her home. His chest swelled with anger. Who in the hell had been in her house the night before? Who had violated what she would have believed was her safe space to terrorize her? And what might they have done if Dillon hadn't shown up when he had?

For the next hour he took care of office business, filling out the work schedule for the next week and reading over reports.

It was just a few minutes after noon when he left his office. "I'll be out until tomorrow morning," he told Annie. "But you know I'm always available on my cell phone."

"And you know I'll keep things running smoothly around here," she assured him.

He smiled at the big, blonde woman. "I know, and I appreciate it." Annie O'Brien was dispatcher, receptionist and all things required to run the office efficiently. She didn't gossip about things that went on here and occasionally she tried to mother him. He didn't know what he'd do without her.

"I'll see you tomorrow," she said. "And tell Cassie I said hello."

"Will do." He left the building and walked back outside where autumn was definitely in the chilly air. Winter would soon follow. Damn, he wanted this case solved long before the first snow flew.

Although he would have liked to head straight back to Cassie's place, he headed his car in the opposite direction so he could talk to Leroy about his aliens. If he didn't, Leroy would be fit to be tied by nightfall.

At least he knew exactly what to expect at Leroy's, and a half an hour of sitting on the old man's porch and talking to him should solve his problem.

Leroy's issue with aliens had begun six months after his wife's death from cancer. They had no children and no family that Dillon knew about. He suspected the man was lonely, and a visit from an old friend broke up the ache of that loneliness.

The Atkinson place was on the east side of town. It was a relatively small spread, where Leroy raised a few cattle for personal consumption and boasted one of the best vegetable gardens in the county.

Dillon's parents had owned the ranch next door to Leroy's, and the couples had been close friends. Dillon had known Leroy all his life. He and his wife had been like a favorite aunt and uncle, and on many nights Dillon played in their living room while the adults had played cards at the kitchen table.

He pulled up in front of the small ranch-style home with the covered front porch. The white-painted house was beginning to show the signs of weathering and the garden had gone to weeds.

Despite the slightly abandoned air of the place, the minute Dillon stepped out of his car the front door opened. Boomer, Leroy's old hound dog, came out first, followed quickly by Leroy.

Leroy's bald head gleamed in the sun as he stepped off the porch to greet Dillon with Boomer at his side. "I've got a fresh pot of coffee. Are you up for a cup?"

"Coffee sounds good," Dillon replied. "I'll just sit right here on the porch with Boomer."

It was their routine that they sat in the deck chairs on the porch when weather allowed. Sitting inside Leroy's aluminum-foil-wrapped living room tended to make Dillon just a little bit crazy.

Dillon eased down in one of the chairs with Boomer at his feet. He scrubbed his fingers behind the old dog's ears and Boomer groaned with pleasure.

"Here we are," Leroy said as he returned to the porch and handed Dillon a steaming cup of coffee.

"Thanks." Dillon took a small sip and then eyed the man in the other chair. "So, what's going on today, Leroy?"

"I'm afraid I got you out here on a false alarm. I suppose I should have called and told Annie not to bother you, but I plumb forgot." He paused to take a drink from his cup and then continued, "I got up this morning and saw another one of them depressions in the grass. It wasn't too big, but I got a little worried that they'd visited my land again."

Dillon knew the "they" Leroy spoke of were aliens. "So, why did you decide it was a false alarm?"

"I went out there an hour later and saw that fat bossy cow laying down right there in the same spot. That's the laziest damned cow I've ever owned." Leroy sighed and looked out in the distance. "I just wish those aliens could manage to bring back my Loretta."

"I know you miss her, Leroy. How long has it been since she passed?" Dillon knew, but he also knew that Leroy wanted to talk about it.

"Four long years. We'd just celebrated our forty-ninth anniversary and were planning a big to-do for our fiftieth, and then that damned cancer took her life." His faded blue eyes radiated his sorrow.

"I'll bet there are times you wished you'd never loved her, and then her absence wouldn't hurt so badly," Dillon said.

Leroy looked at him as if he'd lost his mind. "I wouldn't give back one day with her to ease my pain. I've got forty-nine years of memories with that woman…years of loving and knowing I was loved. No, sir, I wouldn't do a thing differently. Now, speaking of matters of the heart, I heard that you and Cassie Peterson had dinner together at the café."

"We did, but it was just a casual thing," Dillon replied.

Leroy grinned, displaying the empty space where an eye tooth had been. "That's what I thought the first time I took Loretta out to eat." He leaned forward. "You got to watch those cute, sassy women. Just when you think you're in control of everything they go and pull the rug right out from beneath you and you're helpless to their charm."

Dillon laughed. "I'm not too worried about that with Cassie. I'm not even sure she'll be around these parts come winter."

"That would be a damned shame. From everything I've heard about her she's a fine woman. Cass would be proud of her. In the short time she's been here she's taken in a lot of people in trouble, just like Cass did when she hired on all her young cowboys."

Dillon tensed. "What do you remember about them when Cass first hired them?"

"Not a lot. Loretta and I were close to Cass and Hank. We all used to get together about once a week to play cards like we did with your folks. Then Hank got sick and died and we didn't see as much of Cass. She was struggling to keep that ranch going. When she told us she was hiring runaway boys brought to her by some social worker, Loretta and I told her she was plumb crazy, but in the end they all worked out for her."

Leroy leaned back in his chair and took a drink, his gaze speculative as it rested on Dillon. "You think one of those men is responsible for the boys in the grave?" he asked.

"I think it's more than likely," Dillon replied and then told him about what had occurred the night before. He figured that was the talk of the town this morning and the only reason Leroy hadn't heard about it yet was because he hadn't gone to town.

"The world has gone crazy." Leroy shook his head. "Aliens sneaking around on farmland, the young folk living with their parents until they're thirty and the price of groceries enough to break a man. And if that's not enough we've got a blood moon forecasted for tonight."

Old prophecies warned that the blood moon was the beginning of the end times. Dillon wasn't worried about myths and prophecies.

Fifteen years ago a heinous crime had taken place and all indications were that the killer was active once again. If what he believed was true, poor Sam Kelly was the eighth victim. With this thought a new urgency swept through him to get back to the Holiday ranch and Cassie.

"I should probably get on my way, Leroy," he said as he stood.

Boomer released a short howl as if protesting Dillon's parting. "Dumb dog," Leroy said affectionately.

"Thanks for the coffee, Leroy." Dillon handed him his cup and then leaned down and gave Boomer a final pat on the head.

"When are your folks coming back to town for a visit?" Leroy asked as he walked Dillon to the car.

"I'm not sure…maybe Christmas if the weather isn't too bad."

"I miss having them around." Leroy grinned. "We all used to have good times together when you were nothing but a little snot-nosed kid. You remember how you'd always wanted me to whistle 'Yankee Doodle'?"

"You're still the best whistler in the county," Dillon replied with a grin. "And now I'd better get back to work."

With goodbyes said, Dillon got back into his car and headed toward the Holiday ranch. Loneliness was a terrible thing. A hundred times Dillon had tried to convince Leroy that no aliens were visiting his land and it would be okay to take down all that aluminum foil.

But he suspected Leroy was afraid that if there were no aliens then Dillon wouldn't come to visit anymore. The old man didn't seem to understand that Dillon would always drop in to visit with the man who had spoiled him rotten as a child and who had been a close friend to his parents.

Thoughts of Leroy fell aside. He hoped Cassie had taken his advice and had her alarm system on. He definitely hoped like hell she didn't allow any one cowboy into her house. There was safety in numbers and that was never more true than now in her situation.

And that was why he was going to stay with her. He didn't want her alone in that house at night. A security system could be breached, but as long as he had breath in his body he'd do whatever he could to make sure she wasn't the ninth victim of a vicious predator.

Chapter 8

Cassie watched the men working on the wall in the stairway. Sawyer carried out the bad Sheetrock while Brody and Flint McCay fitted the new pieces in.

She'd remained isolated in the house for the morning, other than Will, who had shown up and within half an hour had replaced the pane of glass in the window that had been broken. Right now the house smelled of the apple pie she'd just taken out of the oven, and she was more than happy to say goodbye to the slashes in the wall.

Just knowing the wounded walls would no longer be in the house made her feel stronger and more in control. Was one of these men the one who had chased her into her closet? She didn't know. Cer-

tainly any one of them was strong enough to swing
an ax without even breaking a sweat.

But nothing would happen now with the men in
the house together. She was certain that if one of
them tried to harm her the others would rescue her.
At least that was what she hoped.

When the men started taping and spackling,
Cassie heard her back door open. Oh, crap, she'd
forgotten to set the alarm again when the men had
come inside.

She raced into the kitchen to see Dillon standing
with a duffel bag in hand and a fierce scowl on his
face. "I know…I know, I let the men in to do some
work and I forgot to reset the alarm," she said hurriedly.

"Forgetting to set the alarm could mean the
difference between life or death for you," he said
harshly. "I could have sneaked through this unlocked
door, hidden in one of the rooms and then attacked
you when you were here all alone." Veins popped
out in his neck and pulsed in his jawline. It was obvious he was beyond angry with her.

"I'm sorry, Dillon. I just forgot." She hated to see
him so upset.

"Forgetting is not an option." He drew in a deep,
audible breath and his gaze softened. "Cassie, you
have to take this threat seriously."

"I do take it seriously," she replied fervently. "I
know we're talking about my life here. I'm scared,
Dillon, and I just forgot."

"Hey, Chief, give her a break," Sawyer said as he

entered the kitchen. "This is all new to all of us." His caramel-colored eyes darkened. "We didn't know there was an ax murderer in the neighborhood."

Dillon appeared to relax a bit. "I'm just looking out for Cassie's welfare."

"As we all are," Sawyer replied with a slight up-thrust of his chin.

Dillon sighed and looked at her. "You want me to bunk on the sofa or do you have a spare bedroom I can stay in?"

"When you go upstairs the first room on your right has a couple of twin beds and across the hall is a guest room with a queen bed. Either room is fine with me." She'd been so shaken up the night before she hadn't even thought to offer him one of the guest rooms. Her heart thudded just a little quicker as she thought of him under her roof during the long nights ahead.

"I'll just go upstairs and get settled in." With a curt nod to her and another one to Sawyer, he stalked out of the kitchen.

"I just came in to tell you the others are finishing up with the spackling. It will need to dry overnight, and tomorrow we can sand and repaint it all," Sawyer said.

"Thanks. I really appreciate it," she replied.

Sawyer reached out and touched her lightly on the shoulder. "I just want you to know that he's not the only one who has your back."

"I know that, Sawyer, and I appreciate it." She did know that most of her men would have her back no matter what the circumstances, but it was the one who didn't that scared her.

Within minutes the men were gone and the alarm system was armed. Cassie walked back into the great room and stared up the stairs. She didn't blame Dillon for being angry at her. He was going out of his way to move in here to protect her and she had made a stupid, thoughtless mistake. She couldn't make that same mistake again.

She left the bottom of the stairs and sank down on the sofa. She secretly was happy that Dillon was going to stay with her, not just to protect her, but what better way was there to really get to know a man than to live with him?

Maybe he was a complete slob and she'd find his dirty socks all over the house, or perhaps he was really selfish and self-centered. That would certainly stop the wild pull she had toward him.

And maybe without Dillon on her mind, she could decide once and for all where she wanted to spend the rest of her life. Here she would always be a nothing, a nobody, just as her parents had predicted she'd be.

At least if she returned to New York she'd have a chance to figure out how to really be somebody and prove her parents wrong. It would be nice to have their approval for the first time in her life.

And why, oh, why was she thinking about all these things when it appeared that some nutcase was after her?

She looked up as Dillon came down the stairs.

He smiled at her and she relaxed, pleased that he didn't seem to be angry any longer. "I took one of the twin beds in the room on the right," he said. "I also put my toiletries in the bathroom next to the room. I hope that's okay."

"It's fine, but aren't you going to be uncomfortable in a twin bed?" She eyed his broad shoulders and tamped down an edge of heat that threatened to sweep through her. Dear heaven, what was wrong with her?

"I'll be all right." He sat in the chair opposite her.

An uncomfortable silence grew between them. "I baked an apple pie," she finally said, not wanting the awkwardness to go on any longer.

He smiled, that warm slow slide of his lips that she found incredibly attractive. "I smelled it when I first came inside. It brought back memories of when I was a young boy and I'd come home from school to find that my mother had baked that day."

"Are your parents still alive?" He hadn't mentioned them the night they had gone out to dinner.

"Alive and kicking," he replied. "Seven years ago they decided to sell the family ranch and move into a retirement village in Oklahoma City. My mother is now the social director and my dad works maintenance."

"That's nice. Do you visit them often?" Oklahoma City was only a little over an hour away from Bitterroot.

"I try to drive out to see them about once a month or so."

"Are you an only child?" She was hungry to learn everything she could about him, and this conversation was so much better than one about potential murderers.

"I am. Of course my mother tells me the reason she was a stay-at-home mom and there were no more children was because I was more than a handful. In truth she had three miscarriages after me and so they gave up on the idea of me having a sibling."

"Oh, that's too bad. Do you want children?"

"Definitely. I always thought I'd have a couple by now. But I suppose I need to find a wife before I have those children."

"Why haven't you found a wife yet?" According to what he'd told her, Stacy had left town a long time ago. Cassie was certain that most of the single women of Bitterroot had fantasized about the very hot lawman at one time or another.

"I just haven't found that special woman yet. But I definitely know what I want in a wife."

"And what's that?" She gazed at him curiously and was surprised to discover that she hoped he'd say what he wanted was a mouthy little blonde who could only cook a handful of meals and often smelled of turpentine and paint on the days she was working.

He leaned back in the chair and cast his gaze out the nearby window, and once again a small smile curved his lips. "I want a woman who will build her life around mine, one who wants to bear my children and nurture them and fill the kitchen with the scent of homemade bread and sugar cookies. I need her to support me and this town and be my soft place to fall after a hard day at work."

"Whew, that's a pretty tall order," Cassie replied. And the woman he'd just described couldn't be more different than her. Six months ago cooking for herself was throwing something into the microwave instead of eating out and she'd known nothing about this small town. Even if she lived in Bitterroot for the next ten years, she'd never be the kind of woman he'd just described.

"What about you? Do you want children?" he asked.

"I always thought it would be nice to have children," she replied. "But, like you, I haven't found the life partner I want, mostly because I haven't really been looking."

A husband and a family had been a distant dream for her, but she'd wanted her career first. She still wanted it. She needed to prove to her parents that she wasn't just a failure. But as evening approached and she and Dillon moved into the kitchen to fix dinner, New York was the very last place on her mind.

"What can I do to help?" he asked.

"Maybe you could cut up some lettuce for a salad. I'll put the steaks in the broiler and the potatoes in the microwave." She pulled a couple of potatoes from a bag in the pantry and began to scrub them, all the while trying to ignore the scent of Dillon's cologne that seemed to fill the kitchen.

Dinner was pleasant despite the fact that the potatoes were a little crunchy and the steak was over-done. While they ate he asked her questions about the ranch. She told him about the lucrative contract they had with a major meat packager and that Adam was encouraging her to think about getting into the horse breeding business.

"I'm not ready to jump into anything new right now," she said. "I'm still learning all the ins and outs of the cattle business."

"If you decide to do something with horse breeding, don't forget Abe Breckenridge does a little horse breeding. I'm sure he could answer any questions you might have."

"I just know if he offers me any of his spiced cider to politely decline," she said with a laugh.

She made a short pot of coffee and then cut the apple pie for dessert. She watched him take his first bite. "How is it?"

"Good," he replied and grabbed for a drink of coffee.

She frowned at him and took a bite of it for herself. It wasn't awful, but it was tart…very tart. "It's not good. It needs more sugar or more cinnamon or something."

"It's fine, Cassie," he assured her.

"I was shooting for fantastic, not fine. The problem is Aunt Cass's recipes aren't exact. It's a pinch of this and a handful of that and I guess I just didn't get it right." She released a deep sigh.

"Next time you'll know to add a little more cinnamon and sugar," he replied easily.

"That's right. The next time it will probably be much better," she said optimistically.

"What happens to the ranch if something happens to you?" he asked as they worked side by side to clean up the dishes.

She paused between the table and the sink and stared at him. "I don't know. I never thought about it before."

"So you don't have a will in place?"

"Jeez, Dillon, I'm only twenty-nine years old and in good health. A will is the last thing I've thought about." She continued to the sink and placed the dishes in the bottom and then turned to face him once again.

"Maybe you should think about having a will drawn up," he replied.

"If you're trying to figure out who might profit from my death, the answer is nobody right now, least of all any of my men. As it stands now I suppose that if I die, then the ranch would probably go up for auction and if that's the case Raymond Humes would probably swoop in and who knows, I might wind up selling out to him anyway." She drew in a deep breath. "And this conversation is going to give me heartburn if it continues any longer."

He grinned. "I wouldn't want you to get heartburn, so I guess I'd better change the subject."

"Thank you," she replied.

"However, it is something you need to think about," he said. "And now this topic is over."

For the next fifteen minutes they finished clearing the table and loading the dishwasher, and while they worked Dillon talked about his childhood here in Bitterroot.

"When I was five years old I got mad at my mother and told her I was leaving home and was going to live in the doghouse out in the backyard."

"What did she say?" Cassie asked.

"She helped me move a couple of my favorite toys and a blanket out there. I stayed out there for about an hour and then I got hungry. When I came inside to get a snack my mother said I couldn't eat in the house anymore since I'd moved out."

Cassie laughed. "How long did it take you to move back into your bedroom?"

"About three minutes."

He could have read the ingredients in a bottle of drain cleaner and she would have enjoyed it. His voice was so low, so melodic, it reminded her of the warmth she got when she sipped a shot of whiskey.

With the kitchen clean they moved into the great room, where she sat on the sofa and he on the chair across the room. "Do you want me to turn on the television?" she asked.

"Only if you want it on," he replied.

"I usually turn it on in the evenings just so the house isn't so quiet, but I'm really not a big fan."

"What do you usually do in the evenings?" he asked.

She shrugged. "I read or I paint." *Or I sometimes fantasize about you.* Warmth leaped into her cheeks at this thought.

"Where do you paint?"

"I've pretty much taken over the smallest bedroom upstairs and am now using it as my studio."

"Why don't you take me up and show me? I'd like to see some of your work."

"Really? You aren't just saying that?" she asked with cautious delight.

He smiled. "Cassie, you'll learn soon enough that I always say what I mean."

"Okay, then, come into my parlor, said the spider to the fly," she replied before getting up from the sofa.

He laughed and stood, as well. While climbing the stairs, she was acutely conscious of him just behind her. She suddenly felt shy as she opened the door to the bedroom and ushered him into the workroom.

She never brought anyone up here to see her paintings. She watched him walk over to the easel where her latest work in progress was displayed.

Turbulent gray clouds made up the sky in the picture, and wind was evident in the tall treetops. "I'm trying to capture what it must have looked like the day that the tornado hit this area," she said.

She watched him intently as he stepped closer and stared at the canvas. Was she only fooling herself in believing she could paint? Was that why none of her paintings had sold yet through Mary Redwing's website? He probably hated it and now was struggling for words so he wouldn't hurt her feelings.

Failure. The word rang in her head with a discordant tone. *You're nothing but a disappointment to your father and me*, her mother had told her with her father nodding his agreement. *You'll never amount to anything, Cassandra.*

Dillon turned to look at her and his gaze was soft and filled with a touch of wonder. "Cassie, I'm certainly not an art expert, but I'd say you have a ton of talent." He turned back to the painting. "When I look at this I can feel the wind and I can smell the sulphur in the air. It's such a good depiction of the weather that day just before the tornado hit. It's powerful but it makes me slightly uncomfortable."

"That's exactly what I was going for," she replied as an intense relief blew through her. Something else blew through her, as well…a sweet yearning for him to hold her, to kiss her once again.

He looked back at her and there was a spark in his eyes that drew her closer to him. "Cassie," he murmured. She had no idea whether it was a protest or an encouragement. All she knew was that she was suddenly breathless.

Dillon stared at Cassie and his breath hitched in the back of his throat. The waning sunshine drifted in through the window, turning her hair into sparkly strands like angel hair, but there was nothing angelic in the blue fire that shone from her eyes.

"Cassie…" he said again, unsure why he'd said her name.

She took another step closer to him. "It's been one of those days, Dillon," she said softly. "One of those days where nothing bad has happened and my head is clear and I know exactly what I want."

His chest tightened. "And what's that?" The words whispered out of him.

"You." A hint of uncertainty leaped into her eyes. "Unless you don't want me."

"Oh, no… I mean, yes, yes I want you, Cassie." He wanted her more than he remembered ever wanting a woman.

He scarcely got the words out of his mouth when she was in his arms, and he was kissing her and she was kissing him back. Their tongues swirled together in a dance that had him instantly erect. Under any other circumstance he might be embarrassed by his instant reaction, but all he could think about was Cassie's shapely body pressed intimately against his.

Her mouth was hot and her scent drove him more than half crazy with need. He tore his mouth from hers and stared into her eyes, his heartbeat thundering a million beats a second.

"Are you sure, Cassie?" he asked. "I need you to be completely sure."

She smiled. "I've never been more sure of anything in my entire life." She took his hand and led him out of her workroom and toward the master bedroom.

He was on fire and she was the only woman to put out the flames. They reached her bedroom where the scent of lilac and vanilla was even stronger. She turned to face him and came into his arms once again.

This time when they kissed it was not only with

hot desire, but also with the knowledge that they were going to follow through on that desire.

They kissed for several long minutes and then she stepped back from him. Her eyes glowed in the waning light of day as she grabbed the bottom of her sweatshirt and pulled it over her head.

Her bra was white and lacy and her erect nipples were evident through the wispy fabric. His mouth went dry at the sight of her and he quickly unbuttoned his shirt and shrugged it off. He took off his holster and set in on the nightstand, and by the time he'd done that Cassie was out of her jeans. He caught a flash of white lacy bikini panties before she got into bed and pulled up the covers. His fingers trembled as he pulled a condom out of his wallet and placed it next to his gun on the nightstand.

He kicked off his shoes, peeled off his socks and shucked off his pants in record time, leaving him only in a pair of black boxers as he crawled into the bed with her.

Their lips found each other's again and this time his hands caressed up and down her bare back beneath the strap of her bra. Her achingly soft skin begged to be touched.

It didn't take long for him to want to touch all of her. His fingers nimbly unfastened her bra and she sighed in obvious pleasure when he plucked the bra off her and his hands found her bare breasts.

She rolled over on her back and he tongued first one turgid nipple and then the other. She danced her fingers across his shoulders and onto his back, each touch increasing his need of her.

He wanted to take her hard and fast. Yet he also wanted to take it slow and easy to discover everything there was to know about her body.

"Dillon," she moaned his name as he slid his hand down her flat stomach to the edge of her panties. She arched her hips as if anticipating his touch, and any thoughts he might have had in his mind flew away. There was just him and Cassie and wonderful pleasure.

She helped him take off her panties and he tossed them on the floor next to the bed, leaving her beautifully naked in the purple shadows of night. He kissed her again. His fingers played against the very center of her, making her gasp with pleasure.

"Oh, yes," she whispered as she arched her hips to meet his touch. He slipped a finger into her warm wetness, and her muscles constricted around him.

He knew exactly when she reached her release. Her body stiffened and she appeared to stop breathing. She shuddered and went boneless. Her eyes flew open and she gasped, "Take me now, Dillon. Please... I want you now."

He couldn't get his boxers off fast enough. He got the condom and rolled it on, then poised himself between her thighs. Every muscle in his body trembled in anticipation.

"Yes," she whispered and reached up to him.

She grabbed his shoulders as he slowly eased into

her. He closed his eyes, momentarily overwhelmed by the sweet, hot sensation of being inside her.

He was almost afraid to move, fearing that it would be over before it really began. He drew several deep breaths to center himself and then he truly made love to the woman who'd had him aroused for what seemed like forever.

She met him thrust for thrust, her fingernails biting into his shoulders. They moved faster...more frantic, and his fragile control spiraled away.

His explosive climax rocked through him and he was vaguely aware of her crying out his name as he stiffened against her. Still locked with her, he bent his head down and captured her lips with his.

The kiss was long and sweet and threatened to stir him all over again. When it ended he rolled to the side of the bed, grabbed his boxers and went into the adjoining bathroom.

He turned on the light and stared at his reflection in the mirror above the sink. "What in the hell do you think you are doing?" he asked the man who looked back at him. And why in the hell did he already want to do it all over again?

He had nothing to offer her but a physical relationship. He'd given up on love when Stacy had left him, and allowing himself to develop any real feelings for Cassie would be foolish. How many times did he have to remind himself of these facts?

There was no way to deny that they shared an intense sexual attraction to each other, but he needed her to understand that was all he was willing to give her, and in any case it shouldn't happen again.

He cleaned up and pulled his boxers on, all the while his mind going over the conversation he and Cassie needed to have. He had to make her understand that this had been a one-time deal. He was here to protect her, not to indulge in a hot fling that had no future for either of them.

Stepping out of the bathroom he resolved to talk to her right now, before she got any ideas about what had just happened between them and what it might mean in the days going forward.

While he'd been in the bathroom she'd pulled on a navy blue nightgown and turned on the bedside lamp. Her cheeks were flushed, her lips looked slightly swollen and her hair was in charming disarray. She looked utterly gorgeous, which made the conversation he needed to have with her all the more difficult. Especially when all he really wanted to do was fall back into bed with her.

"Cassie, we need to talk."

"Popcorn," she replied. She slid out of the bed and stood facing him. "I'm in the mood for some popcorn. Why don't I make some and we can build a fire in the fireplace and watch a movie together?"

"Cassie…" he began again.

"Please, Dillon. This was the best thing that has happened to me since I moved to Bitterroot and took over this godforsaken ranch. Don't take it away from me right now. At least give me this one night to feel good."

Her eyes shimmered with the need for him to grant her a stay of execution. Just one night, that was all she wanted right now. Surely he could talk to her about this in the morning and make her understand where he was coming from.

He drew in a deep breath and released it slowly. "What movie are we watching?"

Chapter 9

Cassie stood in the kitchen, the scent and sound of the microwave popcorn filling the air. Dillon was in the great room building a fire in the fireplace.

Dillon. He'd taken her breath away. He'd loved her body like it had never been loved ever. She grabbed the countertop, her knees threatening to weaken as she thought of what she'd just experienced with him.

She'd fantasized about being intimate with him for months and those fantasies hadn't begun to come close to the real thing. He'd been demanding, yet giving. He'd been gentle and powerful at the same time. He'd been exactly what she wanted…exactly what she needed.

The popping of the corn slowed down and she moved to the microwave to take it out. The smell of the wood fire drifted into the kitchen. The house suddenly smelled like winter.

Would she still be here on the ranch when the snow came, or would she be in a cramped New York apartment attempting once again to attain her dream?

Maybe you'll be dead.

The horrifying words jumped into her mind and she consciously willed them away. She refused to think about the reason Dillon was here with her right now. The last thing she wanted to dwell on was thoughts of a killer when her body smelled of Dillon's scent and was still warmed by their lovemaking.

Tonight she just wanted to pretend that he was here because he loved her. She wanted to cuddle in his arms and lose herself in thoughts of what they'd just shared together.

Juggling the popcorn bowl and two bottles of beer in her hands, she returned to the great room to see Dillon standing in front of the fireplace.

Clad only in his boxers, he looked breathtakingly magnificent. The radiance of the fire danced along his broad shoulders, and shadows darted across his muscled back.

He turned and gazed at her, and for a moment she feared he was going to tell her what a big mistake their making love had been. She tensed, but instead he smiled at her. "I didn't think I was hungry after dinner, but that popcorn smells delicious."

She relaxed. "There's nothing better on a chilly fall night than a fire and fresh popcorn and a cold beer." *And a handsome man to cuddle with*, she added mentally. "You sit and I'll put the movie in." She set the bowl and the beers on the coffee table and noticed he'd carried his gun downstairs, and it now sat on the coffee table, as well. She then went to the cabinet that held a vast array of DVD movies. "Have you seen *Married to a Deadly Diva*?"

He quirked a dark eyebrow upward. "Is that the real name of a movie?" She nodded. "Surely your aunt didn't have that in her movie collection?"

"No, it's one of my favorite movies and I brought it with me when I moved here. I think you'll like it. There's lots of gunshots and stuff blowing up in it."

"Okay, I'm game."

She put the movie in and then walked back to the sofa. "Stretch out and make yourself comfortable," she said. "We can be cuddle buddies for the movie." He'd put a glow in her heart and she wasn't ready to let it go yet.

He lay on his side and she lay down in front of him, his body warm and welcome against her back. She pulled the popcorn bowl in front of her, snuggled into him and then the movie began.

She'd already seen the movie before and she found her mind drifting as it played. It didn't help her concentration each time Dillon reached over her to grab a handful of popcorn.

His breath was warm on the back of her neck, and when he laughed the deep sound rumbled in his chest and resonated in the pit of her stomach. There was no question that she felt ridiculously close to him at the moment, both on a physical and an emotional level.

In her former life she would have never taken the time to rest in a man's arms and watch a movie. She'd been too busy chasing her own tail. But this felt right. He felt right and it scared her more than just a little bit.

She didn't know what she was doing. She didn't know what she was doing with him and she had no idea what she intended to do about her life, about her future.

She frowned and focused on the television. She didn't want to overthink things tonight. She just wanted to enjoy the moment because she had a feeling it might never happen again.

Tomorrow in the light of day everything would be different. She'd seen it in his eyes when he'd come out of the bathroom…regret.

She'd known what he'd wanted to talk about when he'd rejoined her in the bedroom. He'd wanted to tell her that they shouldn't have slept together, that it was all one big mistake.

But right now she didn't feel any regret in the arm that hugged her tight against the length of him. She didn't feel remorse in the hand that occasionally stroked her hair and softly roamed up and down her arm.

The movie was almost over when a loud bang slammed the front of the house. She jumped up, her heart in her throat as he vaulted over her and grabbed his gun.

"Stay right here," he said tersely and headed for the entry. She heard him punch in the code. The front door opened and then closed and Cassie froze in place.

All she could think about was the sound of the ax hitting her walls while she'd hidden in her closet. Was the killer back? Was he outside right now? Had he hit the house to lure Dillon out into the night?

Oh, God, it was so dark outside. Dillon might not even see him coming until it was too late. A gun was no good if you didn't see a target.

Fear squeezed her throat, nearly choking her. Another bang sounded and a small scream released from her. What was happening out there?

Imaginary visions flew through her mind... visions of Dillon trying to escape an ax-wielding madman. They were scenes from every horror film she'd ever watched in her life. A sob escaped her. The last thing she wanted was for Dillon to get hurt...or worse.

She moved with baby steps, her legs wooden, so that she could see the front door. When it opened again who would come inside? Dillon or the killer? She held her breath until she was forced to expel it.

The door swam in her vision as tears filled her eyes. She couldn't believe this was happening. She didn't understand why it was happening.

Should she arm herself? Should she run into the kitchen and grab a knife? What good was a knife against an ax? Still, it would be something. Before she could put thoughts to action the front door opened again and Dillon came back inside.

"Oh, thank God you're okay," she cried and ran toward him. She threw her arms around him and held him tight, her frantic heart beating against his steady one.

"I'm okay, Cassie," he said. His skin was cold against hers and she wanted to warm him. "Cassie, everything is fine," he said and gently untangled her arms from around him.

She stepped back from him as her racing heartbeat slowed. "What was the noise?"

"The wind has come up and one of the shutters on the front of the house is loose. That's what is banging," he replied. "Tomorrow when I get back here from work I'll get a couple of nails and take care of it. And speaking of work, I think it's time I call it a night."

"But what about the movie? You haven't seen the end." She tried to get her emotions, specifically the residual fear, out of her head.

"I know how it ends." He turned to the small keypad on the wall and rearmed the alarm. He looked at her once again. "The heroine blows up the bad guy in his car and then returns to her husband, who forgives her for everything."

"How did you know that?" she asked in surprise. "I thought you'd never seen it before."

He smiled, although the gesture didn't quite reach his gray eyes. "I haven't. Fiction is usually pretty predictable. It's real life that isn't. I'll take the popcorn into the kitchen and you can turn off the television and then why don't we both head to bed?"

She put the movie away and turned off the television and together they climbed the stairs. When they reached the landing and the entrance to the first bedroom he turned to her. "I'll probably be gone in the morning when you get up. I'll check in throughout the day and will plan on being back here around suppertime. And you know what you need to do."

She nodded. "Keep the alarm on and don't let anyone inside the house."

"That's right, and now I'll just say good-night." He stepped into the room with the two twin beds.

She wanted to ask him to sleep in her bed, to hold her in his arms while she drifted off to asleep. But whatever warm, cuddly mood they had established before the shutter had banged into the side of the house was gone.

"Good night, Dillon," she replied and then headed down the hallway to her own bedroom.

She crawled into bed and grabbed the spare pillow and hugged it to her chest. It smelled of Dillon's cologne. Fiction was predictable and real life wasn't. His words played in her mind.

She couldn't have predicted that a killer would come after her and Dillon would move in here and they'd make love. She certainly couldn't have foreseen that he'd touch her heart in a way it had never been touched before.

But he wasn't looking for love. She knew with a woman's intuition that he regretted them falling into bed together. She wasn't looking for love, either. She didn't need love in her life; what she needed was to be somebody. She needed to prove to her parents that she was worth something.

She pushed away the pillow that held Dillon's scent and turned over on her back. She stared at the ceiling and focused on her latest painting. Maybe if she added some ochre to the treetops it would emphasize the sensation of the approaching storm.

If she sold the ranch she would have enough money to get an apartment in New York and focus solely on painting. She would be living her dream.

The opportunity was right in front of her; all she had to do was reach out and take it. She'd be back where there were restaurants and shopping, where she could interact with other artists and hopefully build a name.

She could put this dusty Oklahoma town and its cowboys behind her and enjoy being back in the city. So what was holding her back?

He couldn't sleep. The vision of a scantily clad Cassie in Dillon's bare arms had torched a white-hot hatred through him that wouldn't go away.

One peek through one of the great room's windows had confirmed to him that they'd been intimate…were intimate. How else to explain them being half naked on the sofa together?

He'd immediately flashed back to one particularly cold November night years before. He'd been nine years old and his mother had taken him to a cheap motel where he was told to sit in the car and wait for her.

He'd waited for what felt like forever. The icy winter air had drifted into the cracked window in the car's backseat and he'd felt as if he was slowly freezing to death.

He'd finally been unable to stand it any longer. He'd gotten out of the car and approached the motel room. The curtains were pulled, but not quite tight on one side.

He'd peeked in to see his mother and her latest lover in the bed and cuddling while they laughed and watched something on the television.

They appeared to be happy to stay in their positions for another few hours. And why wouldn't they? They were nice and warm.

He'd crept back to the car with hatred burning in his heart, and that hatred was what had kept him warm until his mother had finally returned to drive them home. When he'd complained to her about how cold he was, she'd backhanded him with a vicious slap that had stung for hours.

He now jerked out of bed and pulled on his jeans and jacket. He was too wired up to sleep. The old memories and Cassie's utter betrayal had definitely wound him up. Maybe a little fresh air would help.

It was after midnight and the big house was dark in the distance. Cassie and Dillon were probably in bed together at this very moment. He clenched his fists at his sides. Maybe it was time to rid this town of the chief of police as well as the pretty whore.

"Hey, what are you doing up?"

He turned to see Mac McBride sitting in a folding chair outside his room. "I could ask you the same thing," he said.

"I'm blaming it on the moon," Mac replied and pointed to the full moon that lit the sky.

"I don't know what my problem is. I just thought a couple of deep breaths of fresh air would help me relax and go to sleep."

"Hope it helps. I'm ready to head in and give sleep a chance." Mac stood and grabbed the folding chair. "I'll see you in the morning."

"Bright and early," he replied.

Once Mac had disappeared back into his room, he leaned against his door and drew in deep, slow breaths. His gaze remained on the dark, two-story house in the distance.

Cassie. Her name burned in his soul, creating a sickness inside him that he had to heal. He could be patient. He could wait as long as it took. But he knew the only way for him to get himself well was to kill her.

Chapter 10

One of the most important duties Dillon did as chief of police was to walk the streets of his town and let people see he was present and ready to help them. And this morning he needed the physical activity and interaction with friendly folks more than ever to take his mind off the night before.

Holding Cassie in his arms while they watched the movie had felt like home to him. That particular scene had been one he'd fantasized about for himself long ago. A woman to laugh with, a woman to share with and the warmth of a woman in his arms on a cold night; yes, those had been some of his dreams years before.

But Stacy had stolen his dreams and Cassie wasn't the kind of woman he dreamed about marrying. Besides, he couldn't get in any deeper with her knowing that she might sell out at any given moment.

He now stepped out of the police station door with the intent of walking up Main Street to the café. There he would sit and drink a cup of coffee and then head back to the station.

The wind the night before had ushered in an unusually warm front, probably one of the last of the year. If it hadn't been for the banging shutter the night before, he knew he probably would have spent the night in Cassie's bed. And they probably would have made love again.

Damn the woman for awakening some of the dormant dreams inside him, for making him remember what he'd once wanted from life. He consciously willed thoughts of her out of his head.

There were plenty of people out on the streets enjoying the beautiful day, and he smiled and nodded at people he passed.

"Hey, Chief, how's it going?" Abe Breckenridge stopped to greet him. Next to Abe stood his grandson, Harley. Harley was a handsome seventeen-year-old whom Abe and his wife, Donna, had raised for the last ten years. Dillon had never asked about the son and woman who had given Harley life and then disappeared from the little boy's life.

Dillon smiled at the older man. "It's going, although I think there are some folks in town still trying to recover from your apple cider at Cassie's barn party."

Abe smiled. "It was good. The party was a lot of fun." His smile slowly faded. "Although I was sorry to hear about Sam Kelly and I hope like hell my cider didn't play a part in his murder."

"I don't think alcohol had a thing to do with his death," Dillon replied.

"You got any clues as to who's responsible?"

"I'm working on a few theories," Dillon replied. The last thing he wanted was for the people he served to know that he was nowhere near having anything to help him solve the murder.

"I also heard Cassie had some problems at her place." Abe shook his head. "Heck of a mess."

"It is," Dillon agreed and then smiled at the teenager. "Harley, how are you doing? And why aren't you in school this morning?"

"Teachers' workday," Harley replied. "There aren't any high school classes today."

"Are you keeping your grades up?" Dillon asked.

Harley glanced at Abe. "I have to, otherwise Gramps and Grandma would have my hide."

"And speaking of Grandma…" Abe looked at his watch. "We'd better get moving. Donna sent us into town to pick up a few things and she'll tie my underwear in knots if we don't get back fast enough to suit her."

Dillon laughed. "Then I won't keep you from your errands. I'd hate to be responsible for knots in your underwear."

The three parted ways and Dillon continued on

down the sidewalk, greeting people as he went. He finally reached the café and went inside.

It was just before noon and the place was bustling. "Need a table?" Daisy asked him.

"Not today. I'll just sit at the counter," he replied. Although the scents wafting in the air should have made him hungry, he wasn't. He had too much on his mind to think about food right now.

His short conversation with Abe had put Sam Kelly's murder in the forefront of his thoughts and that, in turn, had intensified the knowledge that Cassie now appeared to be in the killer's sights. And he had no idea who was responsible.

He sank down on one of the counter stools, surprised to see Amanda Wright waiting on customers. She hurried toward him with a smile. "Hi, handsome."

"Hi, Mandy. I thought you were working at the bank."

The pretty, dark-haired young woman wrinkled her nose. "They let me go two days ago, said they were overstaffed." She leaned over the counter toward him and lowered her voice. "Personally I think it was because that old maid Margery Martin saw me in my patriotic bra at the barn dance."

Margery Martin was president of the bank. Even Dillon would admit she was a stuffy, self-righteous old maid. "This is a nice place to work," Dillon replied.

He knew Mandy had a reputation as a wild child and there was nothing Daisy liked better than mothering women like Mandy. Daisy, despite her age and three failed marriages, was still a wild child at heart.

"Daisy has been terrific. Anything new on Sam's murder?" Mandy asked softly, her dark brown eyes radiating a deep sadness.

"Nothing so far," Dillon replied.

"He was such a nice guy. I enjoyed hanging out with him at the party. I really hope you don't think Butch had anything to do with it. Butch knew before we started dating that I'm a big flirt and I told him if he had a problem with it he should just keep riding past my stable."

"Butch seems like a stand-up guy." Dillon had talked to Butch the day after the murder. Dillon suppressed a sigh. It seemed no matter where he went today everyone had murder on the mind.

"Butch is okay for the moment, but I don't think he's my forever man." She flashed him another smile. "I'm still looking for my Prince Charming."

"I hope you find him," Dillon replied. He didn't know a lot about Mandy, but what he did know was fairly tragic. Her mother had died when she was a young girl. Her brother had run off years ago and in recent times her father had become the town drunk.

"At least the hours are more flexible here so that I can be home when my dad needs me. And now, what can I get for you?" she asked.

"Just a cup of coffee."

"Are you sure you don't want some lunch? Daisy's homemade tomato soup and a grilled cheese on Texas toast is the special today."

"Thanks, but just coffee is fine."

Minutes later a steaming cup of java was before him and Mandy had moved on down the counter to attend to other patrons. He sipped his coffee and listened to the hum of conversation going on in the café.

He was just about to relax when Raymond Humes eased down on the stool next to his. "Chief," the old man greeted him with a nod.

Great, just what he needed, Dillon thought. "Raymond," he replied. Dillon had yet to figure out if Raymond had played a part in Sam's death, but he was certainly still high on Dillon's suspect list.

"Beautiful day," Raymond said.

"That it is," Dillon agreed.

"Probably one of the last of the season."

"I think you're right about that," Dillon replied.

"Won't be long before the snow flies and everyone hunkers down in their homes."

"That always makes my job easier," Dillon said.

"Speaking of your job, I've heard through the grapevine you've been out at Cassie's more than once in the last week."

"You heard right. Strange occurrences going on out there, fencing torn down and sheds mysteriously locking themselves. You wouldn't know anything about that, would you?"

Raymond looked at him in surprise. "Why on earth would I know about anything that goes on at the Holiday ranch?"

Dillon gave the man a hard look. "If I find out

your men are behind all this, Raymond, I'll not hesitate to throw you in jail."

Raymond released a rusty-sounding laugh. "What makes you think I have any control over the men who work for me?"

"If they're behind all the things going on at Cassie's ranch, then I suggest you get control over them, because I'll make sure you go to jail right along with them for complicity." Dillon took a drink of his coffee and then continued, "I know you want her ranch, Raymond."

"I haven't hidden my intentions about wanting to buy the Holiday place," Raymond returned. "I don't have to resort to murder or anything else like that. Sooner or later Cassie Peterson is going to go back to the city. She's not cut out for ranch life. She knows when she decides that I'm ready to make it easy on her by taking over the ranch."

At that moment Mandy came over to take Raymond's order, interrupting any more conversation with Dillon. That was fine with him. He finished his coffee and left the café to head back to the office.

He'd had enough town talk for one day. Everyone wanted answers that he didn't have, and the idea of Cassie selling out to Raymond Humes chapped his hide more than just a little bit.

You aren't invested emotionally in Cassie, he reminded himself. She was just a woman he'd slept with and one who currently needed his protection. He shouldn't give a damn where her future was because he was convinced it wasn't with him.

Was it possible one of Raymond's men was trying to terrorize Cassie so that she'd sell out? He might believe that if it wasn't for Sam's brutal death. He knew Humes's men were all kinds of trouble, but murder wasn't their style.

If he could just figure out why Sam had been killed, then maybe he could sort this all out. And if seven skeletons hadn't been unearthed maybe he wouldn't have such a bad feeling in the pit of his stomach.

When he returned to the station and was in his private office, he called Cassie. She answered on the second ring. "I just thought I'd check in," he said. "How is your day going?"

"Okay. Sawyer, Brody and Adam are here finishing up the painting. My wall is back to normal and that makes me very happy. How is your day going?"

He couldn't help the way her melodic voice lifted his spirits a bit. "All right so far. Are you remembering the alarm?"

"Absolutely. I definitely don't want you mad at me again. You look all kinds of mean when you're mad." She laughed and a wave of warmth shot through him at the pleasant sound.

"What's on your agenda for the rest of the afternoon?"

"Once the men are finished I thought I'd check the cookbooks and figure out a good meal to have ready for you when you get here after work."

"Cassie, you know it isn't necessary for you to cook for me," he replied.

"I know it isn't necessary, but it's the least I can do in return for all you're doing for me."

"I'm doing my job," he said. And making love with Cassie Peterson had nothing to do with his work, he told himself. Still, the thought didn't halt the memories of her throaty moans or her body's welcome of him the night before.

"Right. All I need to know is about what time you think you might be here so I can plan the meal accordingly. I'm trying a new recipe. I hope you like chicken."

"I like chicken just fine and I plan on leaving here around five barring any emergencies that might arise."

"Okay, then I'll see you when you get here."

They ended the call and Dillon reared back in his chair. He hated that just hearing her voice, that just talking to her so briefly, changed his mood.

More than anything, he hated that he couldn't wait until five when he could leave work and spend his evening with her.

It was two thirty when Cassie tackled the smothered chicken with potatoes recipe. According to the recipe it had to cook for an hour and a half, so she figured if she got it into the oven by three then she could turn the oven down to warm and it would be ready to serve when Dillon got there around five.

As she peeled potatoes her thoughts were filled with Dillon, as they had been for most of the morning. He seemed to have gone out of his way on the phone to remind her that he was staying with her because it was his job.

If one of the other women in town was in danger would he move in with them? Would he take them to bed and make sweet, hot love with them?

She didn't think so. There was definitely some sort of wild chemistry between them, a chemistry he couldn't deny. Could it be anything more than a sexual attraction? She didn't know, but it was already more than that as far as she was concerned.

She'd just put the chicken in the oven when her phone rang. A glance at the caller ID let her know it was Mary Redwing. "Hi, Mary."

"Congratulations, you sold a painting."

Cassie's heart jumped in wild elation. "I did… Really?"

Mary laughed. "You really did."

"Which one?" she asked.

"Cowboy at Dusk," Mary replied. "A man from North Dakota bought it and his payment went through without a problem. I'll text you his address so you can ship the painting to him."

"Okay. Oh, Mary, I'm so excited!"

Mary laughed. "I hope you're excited enough to keep painting and allowing me to put them up on my website. I have a feeling this is just the beginning for you and I'm so glad we've partnered up."

"Me, too," Cassie replied, her heart still doing happy somersaults in her chest. "I'm working on a new painting right now." She thought of the approaching storm in her latest work. "It's called Imminent Danger."

"Ooh, sounds intriguing. I can't wait to see it."

"I should have it done in the next week. How is Joey doing?" Joey was Tony Nakni's baby with another woman, a woman who had been killed. Tony was one of Cassie's cowboys and through fate he and Mary had found each other and fallen in love. Mary would be the only mother Joey knew.

"He's growing like a weed." Mary's voice was filled with love. "I never knew how wonderful it would be to be a mother."

"I'm so happy for you and Tony and Joey," Cassie replied.

"Thanks. I'll let you go now so you can get to work. I can't wait to get your new painting up for sale on the website."

"Thanks again, Mary. I appreciate the opportunity you've given me."

"No, thank you for the privilege of allowing me to sell them."

"Yes!" Cassie punched the air in triumph once she'd hung up from Mary. Somebody had liked one of her paintings and that somebody had liked it well enough to put their money where their mouth was.

She happy danced around the kitchen table and then raced up the stairs to her workroom. In the closet she had the paintings that Mary had put up for sale for her. She pulled out the one that had sold and set it aside.

Thank goodness when the paintings had first

gone up on the website she'd had a burst of optimism and had bought all the shipping supplies she'd need.

She'd have to cover the painting in Bubble Wrap and then place it in one of the special crates she'd bought for shipping. Her cell phone dinged and she knew it would be the text of the name and address of her buyer from Mary.

But before she wrapped up the sold item, the painting on the easel called to her. Imminent danger, that was what Dillon had said she was in, and the two words were appropriate as a title on her painting. The farm in the picture was in danger of the approaching storm. Maybe she'd just work on it for a little while. She picked up her paintbrush and got to work.

"Cassie? Are you up there?"

Dillon's voice drifted up the stairs.

"Yes, I'm in my workroom." She hurriedly tossed her brush in turpentine. Oh, God, how long had she been up here? As usual, she'd lost all track of time while she'd been painting.

"Looks like you've been busy." Dillon stood in the threshold.

"I sold one of my paintings." Once again happiness danced through her and she ran to him and grabbed his hands. "Mary called me and told me my Cowboy at Dusk sold. I am absolutely delirious with happiness."

Dillon laughed and squeezed her hands. "Congratulations. We should do something special to celebrate. Do you have any champagne in the house? We should at least toast to your success."

She laughed with the pure joy of the moment. "We can have champagne after dinner." Horror swept through her. Dinner. She'd forgotten all about it. "What time is it?"

"Almost six," he replied. "I was a little late getting out of the office."

She dropped his hands and pushed past him. She raced down the stairs and into the kitchen. Grabbing two hot pads she opened the oven door and was met with a wave of heat and the scent of burned chicken.

"Oh, no," she exclaimed as she pulled the baking dish out of the oven and set it on the counter. She tore off the aluminum foil and stared at the overcooked mess. She looked up to see Dillon. "It's totally ruined."

Disappointment overwhelmed the joy she'd felt only seconds before. "I wanted to cook you a nice dinner." She looked down at the meal once again and was shocked to feel tears gathering in her eyes.

Dillon touched her on the arm. "Cassie, it's just chicken," he said softly.

She turned and gazed at him, tears blurring her vision. "No, it isn't just chicken. It's burned chicken and it was supposed to be a good meal for you after a long day at work."

He reached out and dragged a finger gently down her cheek. His gaze was warm as it locked with hers. "Successful artists don't cry over burned chicken. Do you have a pizza in the freezer?"

"Yes, I think there's one."

Once again he touched her cheek. "I think pizza and champagne are a fitting celebration. I'll bake the pizza and you find the booze and that smile you greeted me with when I first walked in."

It was at that moment Cassie realized how very easy it would be to fall in love with Dillon Bowie.

Their celebration took place over pepperoni pizza and champagne. He could tell the minute she'd had not quite enough pizza and a little too much of the bubbly.

Her cheeks flushed a gorgeous pink, her eyes took on the bright sparkle of gemstones and she became even more talkative than usual, which he wouldn't have thought possible.

"I always thought I'd be celebrating my first sale in some fancy art studio and be surrounded by artist types," she now said. "They'd all toast to me and then I'd eat a couple of fancy hors d'oeuvres that I didn't really like and then I'd go back to my tiny half-bare apartment to pray for more sales."

She shook her head, took another sip and then grinned at him. "But this is nice. I'm so glad I got to celebrate my first real sale with you."

"I'm glad to be sharing your celebration," he replied.

"I'll bet your parents gave you huge birthday parties when you were growing up," she said.

His mind shifted gears to stay up with her free-flow conversation. "Yeah, they did. Didn't you have birthday parties when you were little?"

"My parents were workaholics and didn't have time for parties. Besides, my birthday is close to Thanksgiving and they definitely didn't have time for a kid's party while doing a Thanksgiving Day feast for the people at their law firm." She gave him a large, slightly loopy grin. "But it doesn't matter, right? Because we're celebrating my success. Tonight I am somebody."

A knock on the back door stopped any response he might have made. "It's Adam," Dillon said, seeing the man through the window.

"Oops, I forgot that I told him from now on instead of doing morning updates we'd do evening ones when you're here." She jumped up from the table and swayed her way to the back door. It took her two tries to punch in the security code and open the door to allow him inside.

"Adam, we're celebrating," she said cheerfully.

"Did you solve Sam's murder?" Adam asked Dillon.

"No, not yet," Cassie replied before Dillon could open his mouth. "I'm sure he will. He's a brilliant chief of police, but right now we're celebrating because I sold a painting."

"Congratulations," Adam said.

"Thanks." She sat back down at the table and gestured for Adam to join them. "I'd offer you some champagne, but the bottle is empty." She giggled. "Dillon drank it all."

Adam cast Dillon a look of amusement.

"Now, tell me about all the cows news there is to tell," Cassie said.

As Adam gave Cassie his daily ranch report, Dillon listened absently and studied the man. Whenever he was around any of the men who worked on the ranch he found his suspicion that one of them was the killer more difficult to sustain.

Whoever Dillon was hunting, he was good…very good at maintaining a false face to the world. He hid his evil behind guileless eyes and a friendly smile. Or, in the case of Humes's men, behind a sneer and a cocky attitude.

He focused his attention back on Cassie, who was laughing at something Adam had said. God, she was gorgeous. Just sitting across the table from her had him half aroused.

It had touched him deeply that she'd been so upset about the ruined dinner. It was obvious she was only cooking in an effort to please him.

It also broke his heart a little for her that her parents had never given her a birthday party. What kind of cold animals had raised her?

But he couldn't forget what her dream had been for her first painting sale. She'd envisioned herself in an art gallery in New York City. It was just a whimsy of fate that had placed her here in Bitterroot with him, and that same fate was responsible for the fact that they were celebrating her first sale at the kitchen table in the property she'd inherited.

But he hadn't lost track of the possibility that her

subsequent sales would occur in an art gallery in New York City. She was here now, but she could be gone next week. He wished she'd make up her mind already about what her future plans were.

The possibility of her leaving was why it was vital that he not get any more involved with her. He had to protect himself. It had been a mistake to make love to her because he wasn't the kind of man who indulged in meaningless affairs. When he loved, he loved deeply, and he had to stop his feelings for her before he hit the point of no return.

"I think we're good for tonight," Adam said and stood to leave. "I'll check in again tomorrow evening, and congratulations again on the big sale." He nodded to Dillon and then left by the back door.

Dillon got up and reset the alarm. "How about I make a pot of coffee?"

"Coffee might be good. I have to confess that I'm a little tipsy," she said sheepishly.

He grinned at her. "Yeah, I noticed."

"At least I know what to do if I have a hangover tomorrow morning."

"What's that?" Dillon asked while he measured out the coffee.

"Greasy eggs and lots of water."

He turned to look at her. "Really?"

She nodded, her curls bobbing with the gesture. "Halena told me and it really works. I woke up with a terrible hangover after the barn party and she fixed me right up."

"I'd believe almost anything Halena Redwing

said." He turned back to the coffee machine and once it was dripping through he returned to his chair at the table.

"There's leftover apple pie," she said and then giggled once again. "If you like it so tart your cheeks squeeze together and you can't talk for ten seconds."

"It really wasn't that bad," he protested.

She fell silent as he got up once again to pour the coffee. He set her cup in front of her and returned to his chair with his coffee before him.

She smiled at him. "You are such a nice man, Dillon. I just can't figure out why some woman hasn't snapped you up. You must be extremely picky."

"I guess I am," he admitted. "I know what I want and so far I haven't found it yet."

"But you thought you had it with Stacy," she said and then took a drink of her coffee. Her eyes held his gaze intently over the rim of the cup.

"Yeah, I thought I'd found it for a while, but obviously it wasn't meant to be."

She lowered her cup. "Do you believe in soul mates?"

He frowned thoughtfully. "I do. My parents are as in love with each other now as they were when they first got married. They still hold hands and often finish each other's sentences. I believe they're soul mates."

"That's nice." She took another drink of her coffee.

"What about you? Do you believe in soul mates?" he asked.

"I don't know," she replied and stared down into her cup. When she looked up at him again there was a touch of sadness in her eyes. "I'm not sure I believe my parents are soul mates. There were times I even wondered why they stayed married to each other."

"They fought a lot?" he asked.

"No, not at all." A tiny wrinkle appeared in the center of her brow. "They're both highly intelligent and devoted to their law firm. I think the only thing they really have in common is their obsessive need to succeed. They were distant with each other and they were distant with me." She remained still for several long moments, as if reliving something in her mind and then she released a little laugh.

"Sorry, I got sidetracked," she said. "The original question was do I believe in soul mates? I'm not sure. The verdict is still out."

For the next few minutes they drank their coffee in silence. It was a comfortable quiet and he could tell the effects of the champagne were slowly wearing off her.

"Want another cup?" he asked when she'd finished her drink.

"No, I'm good. Why don't we get out of the kitchen?"

There was little to clean up and it took only minutes for the two of them to settle on the sofa. He kept to his own corner, as always acutely aware of her evocative scent and the warmth that radiated from her.

"This has been one of the best days of my life,"

she said. "I thought I had some talent, but there's nothing better than somebody validating it by buying a painting."

"It's a shame you didn't have that fancy art gallery and fellow artists to help you celebrate," he replied.

"Pizza, champagne and you were perfect." Her gaze was warm...too warm on him. "There's only one thing that would make it even more perfect." She leaned toward him, open invitation written all over her face.

"Cassie, please don't look at me that way," he protested.

"What way?" she asked and moved slightly closer to him.

He jumped up and walked across the room to the chair. "Stop looking at me like you want me." Warmth filled his cheeks as he continued to look at her.

"But Dillon, I do want you," she said softly.

"We can't go there again, Cassie." He eased down in the chair and realized the conversation he'd thought to have with her the night before after making love to her needed to happen right now. "Last night was amazing, but we just can't go there again."

"Why not? We're both single and consenting adults and surely you aren't going to try to deny that you're attracted to me." She sat up straight and looked sober as a judge.

"No, I'm not going to deny that. But, Cassie, I'm here for your protection, not to build any kind of a relationship with you. It's not fair to you for me to sleep with you knowing that I have no future plans with you."

She stared at him for a long moment. "What if I'm okay with that?"

Oh, God, the woman was positively killing him. He was trying to do what was best for both of them and she'd never looked as alluring as she did at the moment.

"I'm not okay with that," he replied.

She held his gaze and he was surprised to see a little challenge in the blue depths. "I just want you to know that I can't promise I won't try to change your mind."

"Is that a threat?" he asked with a touch of humor.

She grinned. "A promise. It's definitely a promise." She pulled herself off the sofa. "I think I'll go upstairs and work for a little while before bedtime. I'll just say good-night now."

"Good night, Cassie." He couldn't help but notice there appeared to be extra wiggle in her cute butt as she passed him on the way up the stairs.

He released a deep sigh as she disappeared from his view. He definitely needed to find this killer sooner rather than later.

Chapter 11

Cassie stood at her kitchen window and stared out at the cloudy, gray day. It mirrored her current mood. In the past week life with Dillon had been both wonderful and excruciatingly torturous at the same time.

They'd shared deep, meaningful conversations about philosophical issues, their ideas on parenting and their beliefs on whether ghosts were real or not.

They'd laughed together as they watched movies and they'd shared little tidbits of their day over dinner each evening. They'd even played a mean game of poker one night where he'd managed to win all of the toothpicks they were wagering. But the one thing they hadn't done was intentionally touch.

Oh, they'd brushed shoulders at the kitchen sink and their fingers had accidentally touched reaching for food at the same time. But there had been no kisses, no warm hugs or caresses and it was driving her just a little bit crazy.

She thought it might be driving him crazy, too. She was aware of him gazing at her when he thought she didn't notice. When she did meet his gaze she saw suppressed desire there, darkening his beautiful eyes to a steel gray.

The week had been quiet and she was beginning to wonder how long he would be here. There had been no breaks in the case. He had no leads to follow and she knew he couldn't just stay here with her forever, although there were moments when she thought that might be wonderful.

She released a deep sigh and turned away from the window. She wasn't taking any chances with dinner tonight. In the last week she'd managed to cook a halfway decent pot roast, but had fumbled on other attempts to provide him a good dinner. One night he had surprised her by bringing home a spaghetti dinner from the café.

On the menu tonight was chicken noodle soup and ham-and-cheese sandwiches. She grabbed one of the cans of soup, opened it and then dumped it into a pot on the stove. Thank goodness there was no way to screw up canned soup and sandwiches.

She emptied three cans of the soup into the pot and then turned the burner on medium heat. Dillon should be coming home at any time.

This isn't his home, she reminded herself. And she still wasn't even sure if it was going to be hers for long. She set the table and tried to still the sweet anticipation that filled her as she waited for Dillon to arrive. It was an anticipation she'd experienced every night as she waited for his return after a day of work.

Once again she walked over to the window and stared out into the distance. The view had become so familiar. Outbuildings and pastures and men on horseback going about their daily chores.

There was no question she felt a sense of peace here that she knew she would never find in the city. When she went shopping in Bitterroot, there were no swearing taxi drivers, no squeal of bus brakes and no people jostling or cursing to get to their destination as quickly as possible.

In this town most of the people stopped to pleasantly greet each other and they didn't appear to be in any real hurry to get anywhere. Almost all of them wore friendly smiles on their faces whenever she saw them. Definitely a far different pace than in the city.

Her heartbeat quickened as Dillon's car pulled down the long drive and parked just outside the back door. He got out of the car and once again she was struck by how handsome he was. While her physical attraction to him was off the charts, over the past week she'd become emotionally connected to him, as well.

He spied her standing at the window, and that wonderful slow curve of his lips lifted into a smile that warmed her heart. She returned the smile with a wave.

Was this what it was like to be in a real, committed relationship? This feeling of elation whenever she saw him? This bliss in her heart knowing that he'd be here with her at least for another night?

Was this possibly love? The contentment of talking to him in the evenings? The joy of sharing a simple, burned meal with him? The desire to see his smiles as often as possible?

She hurriedly moved to the door, punched in the code and then opened it to greet him. "Hi."

"Hi, yourself," he replied.

As he swept passed her and into the kitchen, she smelled his familiar scent, and a warmth pooled in the pit of her stomach. "How was your day?" she asked.

"Busy. Somebody robbed the little convenience store on the west side of town sometime last night."

"Oh, no, was anyone hurt?"

"Thank God the store was closed at the time." He walked over to his chair at the table, pulled his black cowboy hat off his head and sank down.

"Was a lot of money stolen?" She walked over to the cabinet and began to pull down bowls and plates.

"No money, just booze and snacks and candy bars. I have a feeling within the next week or so there are plans for a big teenage gathering in some pasture."

"So you think it was kids who broke in." She set the table as he told her more about the crime that had taken place sometime after midnight.

"Yeah, there had to be more than one to carry all the stuff outside."

"Aren't there security cameras in the store?" she asked.

"There are, but some wise guy threw a cowboy hat over it so it didn't show who was inside and doing the damage."

She carried the ham and cheese and bread to the table. "That stinks," she replied. "Do you have any ideas who might be responsible?"

He grinned. "I have a very specific idea. I recognized the cowboy hat. It belongs to Abe Breckinridge's grandson, Harley." He shook his head. "Dumb kid."

"Oh, Abe and Donna are going to be absolutely heartbroken. Have you already talked to them?"

"Yeah, right before I came here. I spent most of the day processing the scene and trying to find some evidence that would point to another guilty kid."

"Did you find anything?" she asked.

"No, and when I spoke to Harley he wouldn't give up any other names, although I have my suspicions as to who else was involved. Jim doesn't want to press charges. I tried to change his mind, but he just wants to either get his merchandise back or be paid for the stolen stuff. He doesn't want to ruin Harley's life forever for some stupid teenage crime."

"That's nice of Jim." She got the soup from the stove and ladled it into the bowls.

"Jim, Abe, Harley and I are going to sit down first thing in the morning and work out all the details. I figured a night of Abe hammering at Harley would probably convince Harley to tell me who broke in with him and where the stolen stuff is located. I needed to knock off for today so I could get back here before dark."

She frowned. "I hate that this is interfering with the way you do business," she said. She carried the soup pot back to the stove and then joined him at the table.

"Don't worry about it," he replied. "I knew what I was signing up for when I decided to stay here."

But she did worry about it. It bothered her while they ate dinner and small talked. It continued in her thoughts as they cleaned the kitchen and then moved into the great room to watch television.

Was she really in danger or had the axman only meant to frighten her into selling the property to Raymond Humes? Was what had happened to her really connected to the crime that had taken place here fifteen years ago?

And then there was the fact that every second, every minute she spent in Dillon's company only made her want to spend more time with him. And that confused her.

If she was going to leave Bitterroot to head back to New York she had to make a decision in the next week or two at the very latest. She just couldn't put it off any longer than that.

At eight o'clock Adam knocked on the door to give her the daily report. He had nothing new to report other than Clay Madison, the ranch's resident

Romeo, had hit his head in the stables and suffered a mild concussion.

"The doctor told him to stay in bed and rest tomorrow," Adam said.

"He needs to let me know if there's anything I can do for him," Cassie replied. She absolutely hated it when any of her men were sick or got hurt.

"You know Clay. He has half a dozen women in town to bring him anything he needs if he asks them."

Cassie laughed. She knew Clay's reputation as a ladies' man. "Just keep me posted on how he's doing and tell him I'm thinking about him."

"Will do," Adam replied.

Minutes later Cassie and Dillon were once again alone in the house. More than once she felt his gaze lingering on her. Even though his mouth said one thing, she felt his longing for her.

She knew if she pushed him, if she really set about seducing him, they would once again wind up in her bed making love. But as much as she wanted him tonight she felt strangely vulnerable.

She didn't see how this all ended. How long was reasonable for him to stay here? He'd already been here well over a week. She really had no idea how big a burden it was for him to be here with her.

Didn't he have things to do at his own home? Wouldn't he be spending his downtime far differently if he wasn't babysitting her?

As they watched a crime drama show on television her mind refused to quiet. Over and over again she found herself gazing at Dillon. He looked tired. He was really working twenty-four hours a day now with his regular duties as chief of police and then his duty here on top of it.

Maybe she should take Nicolette up on her offer and move in with her. As much as she'd hate not being in her own home, it would ease things for Dillon. But then there was the worry of the danger following her to Nicolette and Lucas's place. There was no way she could take that risk.

Or maybe there was another answer.

She suddenly thought of the handgun she'd found in a case in her aunt's closet. When she'd first found it she'd been horrified and had quickly put it back on the shelf.

Maybe it was time she got it down. Maybe it was time she took a stand on her own. She glanced at Dillon once again and her heart squeezed tight.

If she went through with the plan that had just popped into her head, then it would be the beginning of the end of his time here with her.

She could either be the victim and continue to be a burden to him, or she could stand on her own two feet and be strong, but once again be alone.

She knew what the right thing to do was; she just hoped she was strong enough to live with the consequences.

"I want you to teach me to shoot a gun."

Dillon turned and looked at Cassie. "What gun?" he asked in surprise.

"I found a gun when I first moved in here that must have belonged to Aunt Cass. I want you to teach me to shoot it so I won't have to be a burden to you any longer." For the first time since he'd moved in, he couldn't read the expression in her eyes.

"Cassie, I really don't think that's a good idea," he protested.

She leaned forward. "It's the only idea that makes any kind of sense in this whole mess. Dillon, if I know how to shoot a gun, then I can protect myself and you won't have to be here anymore."

Dillon frowned. It was a terrible idea. He knew the statistics of how many homeowners were killed with the very gun they had purchased for self-protection.

"What if the killer is one of your own cowboys? Would you really be able to look one of them in the eyes and pull the trigger?" he asked.

"If he had an ax in his hand? Absolutely." She lifted her chin. "Dillon, we can't go on like this indefinitely. It could be weeks—even months—before he makes a move again."

His frown deepened as he continued to gaze at her. He didn't think it would be weeks. He believed whoever had come after Cassie would be half-crazed with his need to finish the job he'd attempted and botched. But that was just his guess.

Hell, he hadn't been able to get a handle on the killer so far. What made him think he knew what the man might be thinking now?

"I still think it's a bad idea," he replied.

"Well, I think it's a great idea, and if you won't help me then I'll just get one of my men to teach me how to use a gun." Once again her chin thrust upward in what he now knew was a stubborn defiance.

"You can't live the rest of your life here, dividing your time between your work in town and me. We have to be real here, Dillon. How long do you really think this little arrangement is going to last?" Her voice was now soft. "I need to be proactive about my own safety. I need to let you off the hook."

He knew the best thing for his own mental health would be to run as fast and as far as he could get from her. The last week had been sheer torture. He'd wanted her again every night when he went to sleep in the twin bed.

Her scent haunted him and the memory of their lovemaking had tormented him in the form of erotic dreams. They were all kinds of wrong for each other, but being here with her, enjoying laughter and food and simple conversation, had felt so right.

However, he wouldn't allow his need to escape from her to dictate his actions. He had to think like a professional and not like a man. There was no way in hell he was leaving her here to potentially square off against a vicious killer all alone. Maybe it would be good if she knew how to use a gun.

Most of the women in the town of Bitterroot, especially those who lived on the ranches, were fairly proficient with a weapon. Of course big Cass Holiday had always preferred her bullwhip to a gun.

"You have a place that's good for target practice?" he finally asked.

She sat up straighter. "I know the men use one of the lower pastures for shooting."

"Tomorrow afternoon," he replied. "I'll plan to get off work around two and we'll go to the pasture and see what I can teach you."

She gave him a look of gratitude. "Thank you."

It was only later in his little twin bed that he wondered if Cassie realized how strong she really was. He knew from their many conversations that her parents had made her feel inadequate and had basically written her off as a loser.

That broke his heart more than a little bit for her. He'd always known that whatever he would have chosen to do with his life, as long as it wasn't immoral or illegal, his parents' love and support were behind him.

There was no question that this drama that had appeared in her life was testing her, and he hoped and prayed she found the strength and self-confidence to rise to whatever challenges faced her in the future.

It was just after two the next afternoon when he pulled down the drive and saw her standing at the window, a smile of welcome on her pretty face.

He liked seeing that smile first thing after work. No matter what he'd faced at work, that smile made everything better.

As he got out of the car she opened the door to

greet him. "Did you have any trouble taking off this afternoon?"

"I've been working without a day off for so long I figured I owed myself an early day." He approached where she stood on the porch. There was nothing of a city girl apparent today. She was clad in a pair of jeans and a long-sleeved flannel blue plaid shirt. Instead of dainty heels on her feet, she wore a pair of cowboy boots.

A little frown tugged down in the center of her forehead. "I'm pretty sure teaching me to shoot isn't high on the list of what you'd like to do on your day off."

He touched the end of her nose with his finger. "And I can't think of anything I'd rather be doing." It was true. He'd actually looked forward to spending the afternoon with her and it didn't matter what they had planned for the day's activity.

Her frown disappeared. "I got Aunt Cass's gun from the closet and there was also a box of bullets. It's all on the kitchen table."

"Then let's go have a look at it." He would indulge her in this…but he also knew that after a couple of hours shooting bullets in a pasture, he wasn't about to leave her here all alone.

The gun was a thirty-eight special in pristine condition. He seriously doubted if it had ever been fired. For the next hour he schooled her on gun safety and showed her how to load and unload the weapon.

She was a quick learner and asked questions that

let him know she was taking this all very seriously. She needed to; gun safety was nothing to joke about.

They didn't leave the table until she'd become familiar enough with the gun that he felt comfortable. He ran upstairs and changed into a pair of jeans, a pullover shirt and grabbed his black cowboy hat and then they headed outside.

"The pasture is a ways off. Let's ride," she said and gestured toward the stables when they walked out the back door.

He looked at her in surprise. "I didn't know you could."

"Forest Stevens taught me." Forest had worked for Cassie at the time the skeletons had first been unearthed. While the investigation had been unfolding he'd fallen for Patience Forbes, the forensic anthropologist who had been working the site. He and Patience were now living their happily-ever-after together in Oklahoma City.

It was a perfect day for a horseback ride. There was no wind and the late-afternoon sun was warm on his shoulders. She pointed him to a chestnut mare in one of the stalls. "That's Prancer. We keep her for guests to ride."

While he saddled up the mare, she went to another stall and did the same with a black horse named Twilight. "I was terrified of horses when I first got here, but Forest was so patient with me." She mounted the horse. "He broke Twilight just for me and trained us both at the same time. I miss that big cowboy. He was definitely one of the good guys."

As they left the stables Dillon shot a wary eye around the area. Several of her men were on horse-back in the distance and others were digging out an old tree stump near the barn.

It looked like a normal day on the ranch and he forced himself to relax and take in a deep lungful of the clean Oklahoma air. The horse felt good beneath him as they rode side by side at a leisurely pace.

It had been too long since he'd ridden. He had his own horse, but most of the time it was a neighbor who took care of the animal and rode him while Dillon was busy working. For the past couple of months Dillon hadn't had a real opportunity to enjoy riding.

She shot him a smile and it warmed even the darkest places in his soul. "Feels good to be out of the house," she said.

For the first time he realized how really difficult the past ten days had been for her. Cassie was by nature a very social woman. Being cooped up in her house alone for these many days had to have been difficult for her.

"It's another beautiful day," he replied.

"It's supposed to get really cold by the end of the week," she said.

After that they rode in a peaceful silence. They passed the pond where Cassie's cowboy Dusty Crawford had fished out the skull of the seventh victim in the mass graves. Originally it was thought that there were only six skeletons, but when Patience Forbes finished there were six full sets of bones and another one missing a skull and fingers.

The skull had been pulled out of the pond, but the finger bones were still missing. He doubted they would ever be found. He consciously willed himself not to dwell on that now.

Instead he turned his head to glance over at Cassie. She had her face slightly raised to the sun and, dammit, but she looked like a woman who belonged on the back of a horse. She rode with a natural ease, her hips relaxed and swaying in the saddle with the motion of the horse.

She glanced over and caught him staring at her. "You look good on a horse," he said.

"I enjoy riding."

"There won't be much of that if you decide to return to New York."

"I know." A shadow flashed in her eyes and she turned away.

They continued on and silence rose up once again, this one weighty and a bit uncomfortable. Had he said that to make her think about what she would be giving up, or had it been to remind himself that her future might not be here?

The Holiday land was vast. They passed a pasture where black Angus cattle stood watching them as they rode by. Several cowboys on horseback waved to them from the distance and they both waved back.

They continued to ride and eventually he and Cassie reached an area of pasture that was obviously set up for target practice.

Bull's-eyes were tacked to large bales of hay and

a pile of empty beer bottles awaited setup. Behind and to one side of the hay bales was a wooded area.

They dismounted when they were still some distance away and tied their horses to the wooden fencing nearby.

"Won't they be afraid of the gunfire?" he asked.

"No. All of our horses are trained not to respond. Mac McBride took over working with the horses when Forest left and he's been great."

She flashed him a cheeky smile. "Now, let's get serious. You need to make me a kick-ass kind of cowgirl with a gun."

Dillon stifled a groan. He just hoped he wasn't making a huge mistake and she wound up shooting him or herself by accident.

For the next two hours he worked with her. He showed her how to aim through the site, how to gently squeeze the trigger and how to compensate for the kickback. He again explained to her about the safety lock and how important it was to make sure it was off when and if she ever needed to grab the gun and fire.

It took her a dozen bullets before she finally hit the outer edge of the target. She squealed with excitement. "I did it. I hit the target," she exclaimed. "I'm almost a sharpshooter!"

She set down her gun, grabbed his hand and then whirled him around in a circle so fast his head spun. Or was it her laughter and closeness that made his head spin and his breath catch in the back of his throat?

She stepped away from him and picked up her

gun in her hand. "Now I want to hit the very center," she said with grim determination.

She stepped up and readied herself for another shot. Before she could pull the trigger a crack resounded and the dirt near her feet kicked up.

For a split second Dillon's brain refused to make sense of it, but then his brain screamed. Somebody had just shot at them. He launched himself forward at Cassie.

"Wha—" She didn't get any more out of her mouth as he hit her and took her down to the ground, his body covering hers.

"Stay still," he commanded her. He narrowed his eyes and tried to discern exactly where the shot had come from. He had no idea what had happened to her gun when he'd dropped her, but he clasped his firmly in his hand.

Another crack of gunfire and more dirt kicked up. Close...too damned close. This time Dillon was able to determine that it came from the wooded area on their left. He returned fire, but saw no specific target in view.

His heart pounded and yet he was vaguely aware of Cassie's fluttering heartbeat and frightened gasps beneath him. He hadn't expected this. He had been in no way prepared for this particular new brand of danger. If only he could catch a glimpse of where exactly in the woods the person was. He cursed as yet another round smacked into the ground.

They were sitting ducks, with no real cover to find. Even if he could somehow manage to maneuver them behind the hay bales, there was no guarantee they'd be safer there. Besides, at the moment the hay bales looked like they were a million miles away. But sooner or later the shooter was going to get lucky and one of his bullets would count.

Chapter 12

Cassie fought hard to hold in the hysterical screams that tried to release from her. In the last ten days she'd imagined her own death a hundred times, but it had always been with an ax, not with a bullet. And in any scenario she'd imagined Dillon had never been in the path of that death.

But now he was on top of her, a shield to protect her and risking his own life for hers. She wanted to tell him to run, that the target was her, not him. She needed to beg him to save himself, that the town of Bitterroot needed him and nobody really needed her.

Still, even thinking these things she clung to him, terror chasing through her as the gunshots kept coming. Who was behind the gun? And why...oh, why was this happening?

Another bullet kicked up dirt just in front of them and this time her scream released from her. She quickly clamped her mouth closed, knowing a screaming woman would only distract Dillon.

"Dammit," Dillon said. "I can't see him." He fired another shot.

Shouts sounded from the distance, along with the noise of pounding horse hooves. She nearly cried out in relief as she peeked out from under Dillon and saw Mac Mcbride, Flint McCay, Dusty Crawford and Tony Nakni riding hard and fast toward them.

The four cowboys had their guns pulled and it was obvious they were riding to the rescue. They circled her and Dillon. "Where's the shooter?" Tony cried.

Dillon pointed toward the woods and Tony headed in that direction. Dillon got up and pulled her up and against him. "Come on," he said. "We'll get you on your horse and the men can ride back to the stables with you. Get inside the house and lock the doors."

"But what about you?" she asked worriedly. He couldn't stay out here. Those bullets had not just tried to find her, but had been aimed at him, as well. Even with her gone he might still be in danger.

"I'll be along later," he replied. His jaw was set, and his eyes were narrowed and a harsh shade of dark gray. "Go on, Cassie. Get to safety."

"Come on, Cassie, I'll take you in and Mac can get Twilight," Dusty said. He shifted his position just off the back of the saddle and then held out an arm to her. She looked at Dillon one last time and then grabbed Dusty's arm and pulled herself into the saddle in front of him.

She leaned back in Dusty's arms as he galloped toward the stable. The shots had stopped and she desperately hoped that Tony and Dillon had apprehended the shooter.

Let this be the end of it, she prayed. Let today be the end of the madness. Hopefully before nightfall the killer would be in a jail cell and they'd have answers not only to the who, but also to the why.

Dusty took her straight to the back door, where he helped her down and then waited until she locked herself inside. What kind of a hotshot was she? She didn't even know what had happened to her gun in the melee.

What she did know was that Dillon's first instinct had been to protect her, and hopefully he would return safely. She stared out the window, her heart beating a thousand miles a minute.

What was happening right this minute? Was Dillon still in danger? Were her men? She prayed they all returned safely. She wanted the bad guy caught so badly. She wanted this all to end right this minute.

Even though her heart ached just a little bit to know the solving of the mystery would cast Dillon out of her life, she also knew how important it was to solve not only Sam's murder, but also the crime that had occurred so long ago.

Minutes ticked by. There was not a person in sight as far as she could see. Where was Dillon? And where were any of her men? What was taking so long? The minutes turned into an hour and still she stood at the window, her heart in her throat as she waited to find out what had happened.

She gasped in relief when finally she saw Dillon and Tony riding together toward the stables with her horse following behind Tony. She swallowed her disappointment at not seeing somebody tied up and arrested with the two. Still, her joy at seeing Dillon unharmed far outweighed the disappointment.

The two men disappeared into the stables and then minutes later Dillon reappeared and walked to the back door. He barely got inside before she was in his arms and weeping.

"It's okay, Cassie," he said, his breath warm against her ear. "You're safe here."

"I'm not crying over me, you big lug. I was terrified for you," she managed to say between sobs. "I don't know what I'd do if anything bad happened to you."

He tightened his arms around her. "The good news is we're both okay." He released a deep sigh. "The bad news is I didn't get him." She felt the new tension that filled his body.

"What took you so long to get back here?"

"Come on, dry those tears and let's go sit on the sofa." He led her into the great room. Before he sat he pulled not only his gun and set it on the coffee table, but also hers, as well.

"I wondered what happened to that," she said.

"I think we need to work on your responses to danger," he said.

"You think?" she replied drily. She scooted closer to him.

"After Dusty got you out of there I rode into the woods to see if I could find out exactly where the shooter was positioned."

"Did you find the spot?"

He shook his head and a knot in his jaw pulsed with what she knew was his frustration. "After we checked the woods I told Flint to get all your cowboys into the dining room as quickly as possible. When they were there, I checked all of their guns to see if any of them had been fired recently."

"I'm assuming none of them had, otherwise you'd be booking somebody into jail instead of sitting here with me."

The knot of tension in his jaw pulsed a little bit faster. "You're assuming right. Whoever this is, he's good and he's smart."

"And you still believe it's one of my men?"

His gaze held hers intently. "I do, Cassie. Those shots came from your own property."

"Somebody else might have gotten on my land," she replied without much conviction. As much as she hated to believe it, she had to admit to the very real possibility that one of her men was the killer. "I think it's safe to take Dusty, Flint, Mac and Tony off the list of suspects."

"And I'm not looking at your two new hires too much," he added. "But that still leaves eight men."

"Clay has a concussion and was supposed to be in bed."

"That doesn't take him off my list. He could have easily gotten out of bed and left his room without anyone else seeing him. None of the remaining eight are off my list." He pulled his cell phone out of his pocket. "And then there's Cord Cully. What do you really know about him?"

"Not much," she admitted. Anyone would say that Cord, aka Cookie, was a fantastic cook and provided healthy, filling meals to the men. He was also a loner who kept to himself. "I know Aunt Cass hired him soon after she had most of the young cowboys working for her."

"You ever have any problems with him?"

"None. I pretty much stay out of his way and let him do his thing."

He released a sigh. "I'm going to call in a couple of my deputies to go through those woods more thoroughly. Even finding a footprint would be helpful."

She leaned her head back against the sofa as he made his call. Who was the killer? Clay, with his sparkling blue eyes and charming smile? Sawyer, who always seemed to have her back? Adam, who had been a kind and patient teacher? Or maybe Brody, who was always the first one to step up when there was extra work to be done? Her mind continued to think of the rest of them.

Nick Coleman was now happily married and no longer lived on the ranch, but he continued to work here. What about Jerod, who she knew spent some of his spare time working with kids at the community center? Wasn't there a serial killer in real life who had dressed up like a clown to entertain children?

"Will you be all right here while I go back outside with my men?" His voice pulled her out of her troubled thoughts.

"Of course," she replied. She'd be okay because she had to be. He had to follow up to see if he could find clues that might lead to identifying the guilty.

Within twenty minutes he was gone. Cassie went into the kitchen and busied herself making coffee and sandwiches that she'd told Dillon the deputies could enjoy after their hunt through the woods.

It felt good to do something active and not dwell in her own head. She was still having trouble believing that somebody had actually shot at them that afternoon.

If the shooter managed to kill Dillon with a bullet would he have then come after her? She knew with a horrifying certainty that the answer was yes.

There wouldn't be any more shooting practice for her. Now that they knew the killer didn't shy away from shooting a gun, she had a feeling she wouldn't be leaving the house again anytime soon.

She'd become a prisoner in her own home and for the first time a rich anger filled her. This was her ranch, dammit, and somebody was playing deadly games with her.

There was no way she was leaving here until this homicidal maniac was caught. As long as he was focused on her, then Dillon might have a chance to catch him. With her absence from here he might go dormant again and never get caught. He could continue to murder more people.

She had no idea what she had done to warrant a killer's attention, but at this point it didn't matter. The murderer had to be caught.

It was just after dark when the men came in. Dillon walked in first with Juan Ramirez and Ben Taylor close at his heels. "Nothing," Dillon said in disgust, answering her question before it left her lips.

"Sit down and get something to eat," she replied. "Juan…Ben…coffee?"

"Sounds good," Juan replied.

"Yeah, it does," Ben added. "Thanks."

Cassie poured them all a cup. If there was one thing she'd learned about Dillon it was that he never turned down a cup of coffee.

They helped themselves to the sandwiches and potato chips she'd set on the table and then she leaned with her back against the counter as they ate and talked.

They rehashed everything that had happened since they'd been called out to the ranch because of Sam's murder. Cassie listened to them and a knot of tension formed in the center of her chest, along with a new dose of anger.

Who had killed those seven young men? Who was after her now? And when would they get those answers? Her reaction to the shooting that afternoon felt slightly odd. Other than the few tears she'd shed when she was relieved to see Dillon unharmed, she hadn't cried about it at all.

A month ago she would have curled up in her bed and wept her eyes out. At the first sign of danger she would have thrown her clothes in a suitcase and boot-scooted it right out of town.

But she didn't want to leave yet. She definitely wanted to see this thing through. Her gaze lingered on Dillon. Was it the mystery she wanted to see through or the crazy, wild feelings she had for him? She didn't know the answer.

It was almost eight when Juan and Ben got up from the table. "Cassie, thanks for the sandwiches," Juan said.

"Yeah, appreciate it," Ben added.

"It was nothing," she assured them.

"You remind me so much of your aunt," Juan said. "This was something she would have done."

Cassie looked at him in surprise. "Thanks. I'll take that as a compliment."

"You should. She was a terrific woman," Juan replied.

After the men left, Cassie cleaned up the few dishes and then joined Dillon in the great room. He sat on the edge of the sofa, a deep frown cutting across his forehead.

She sank down next to him. "You're obviously having dark thoughts if your frown is any indication."

The frown smoothed out and he shook his head. "I was just thinking about how much I've underestimated this particular enemy. So far he's done everything right to keep himself hidden from view."

"Have there been any murders in the past in town that weren't solved?" she asked, wondering if this man could be tied to other crimes.

"None," he replied with a sigh. "The only evidence I have is that damned ring that was found, and it might not belong to the killer at all. It could have been on one of the victims when they were dumped into the grave."

She placed her hand on his thigh. "Don't get discouraged, Dillon. I know you're going to get him."

He smiled at her, but the smile lasted only a minute and didn't quite lift the shadows in his eyes. He pointed to her gun on the coffee table. "You know there won't be any more target shooting."

"I'm not eager to have a repeat of today and I'm assuming having a picnic in the pasture is out, too."

His eyes lightened to a soft dove-gray. "A picnic in the pasture sounds great right about now, but we'll have to postpone that fun for a while."

She suddenly wanted a picnic with him. She wanted to sit on a red-checkered tablecloth down by the creek with a light summer breeze playing across them. They'd eat cheese and fruit and drink champagne out of paper cups then make love under a beautiful Oklahoma moon.

"Cassie?"

His deep voice pulled her out of her happy thoughts. "Sorry, I was just thinking about that picnic."

"You do know I don't want you to leave this house for any reason. The gunfire this afternoon changed everything. I expected a man with an ax and now he's an even bigger threat because it's obvious he can change his modus operandi." His frown and darkened eyes were back.

She squeezed his lower thigh. "Dillon, you're doing the best you can. Hey, you must be doing something right. I'm still alive."

"I want to make sure you stay that way." He leaned forward and picked up her gun. "I want you to put this in your nightstand next to your bed. If for any reason somebody gets through me to come after you then you need to grab it and shoot. Pull the trigger all the way back and aim for his chest or belly. Don't shoot to wound, Cassie. Aim for center mass and shoot to kill."

She pulled her hand away from his thigh. "You just scared me," she said softly.

"I want you to be scared," he replied. "Scared will keep you from taking any chances."

"Oh, trust me, I'm not taking any chances. But I don't want to think about anyone somehow getting through you to get to me. I told you before. I couldn't stand it if anything happened to you."

His gaze held hers and in the depths of his eyes she saw the same emotion she'd often seen in his over the last ten days…desire and want.

She'd never longed for a man as much as she did at this moment. A warm rush of heat swept through her and pooled in the very center of her. She wanted to reach for him, but she was afraid that he'd rebuff her, and he didn't reach out for her. Instead he thrust her gun toward her.

"Why don't you take that upstairs and maybe we should call it a night. Even though it's early I feel like this has been a very long day," he said as he broke eye contact with her.

She took the gun and did as he'd asked. She trudged up the stairs with a weariness she hadn't felt minutes before. For crying out loud, she'd survived a gunman's attack, but her heart hurt just a little because Dillon didn't want to take her to bed. What on earth was wrong with her?

Once in her room, she placed the gun in the top drawer and her cell phone on top of the nightstand. Then she sat on the edge of the mattress, unsure what to do next. Dillon had to be exhausted, but a restless energy whirled around inside her, letting her know sleep wouldn't come easily.

She could always paint a little before bedtime, or maybe she should clean out the top of her closet. She eyed the mish-mash of items all stacked haphazardly on the top shelf.

Maybe that wasn't such a good idea tonight when Dillon was trying to get a good night's sleep. She was sure there was going to be a lot of crashing and cursing when she finally decided to tackle that job.

Maybe she'd just spend the rest of the night before sleeping by resuming her reading of her aunt's journals. With this thought in mind she got up to get her nightshirt out of one of the dresser drawers, but before she could get more than one foot in that direction Dillon appeared in her bedroom door.

"I just wanted to tell you good-night," he said.

"Good night, Dillon."

He remained standing in the doorway. "Cassie," he whispered and his features filled with naked hunger. She wanted to jump up and reach for him, but she didn't. This time he had to want her enough to come to her.

And he did.

He stalked across the room and pulled her into his arms. His demanding lips plied hers with a fiery heat as his hands gripped her hips and pulled her tightly against him.

Instantly she was on fire. She ripped at the buttons of his shirt, wanting to feel his smooth muscled nakedness. His mouth left hers and she threw her head back as he nibbled behind her ear and down her throat.

"I was so afraid for you out there today," he murmured. "I was so afraid that he'd get to you."

Surprise winged through her. She framed his face with her palms. "But he didn't. We're here, Dillon, and we're both okay." She barely got the words out of her mouth before his mouth took hers again.

When their kiss ended again, they undressed in a frenzy and fell onto the bed. Hot kisses...even hotter caresses, they moved together like longtime lovers.

He knew exactly where to kiss, where to touch, to ratchet her desire higher and higher. He teased and tormented her, licking first one of her nipples and then the other while his fingers caressed her inner thighs.

By the time he finally caressed her where she

wanted him to most, she practically screamed with the intense release that washed over her.

He was ready to take her, but she wanted to tease and torment him like he had her. She pushed him onto his back and kissed him on the neck, across his broad chest and down his muscled stomach.

He hissed his pleasure as he whispered her name over and over again. He was hard, yet velvety soft, and before she could really torment him like she wanted to he rose up and rolled her to her back.

He took her fast and furiously and it was just the way she wanted it. She met him thrust for thrust. It was an affirmation of life that she knew they both desperately needed after death had come so close to them.

When they were finished he kissed her with a tenderness that swelled her heart. And she felt like crying because she knew she was in love with a man who had already told her he wasn't looking for love.

Chapter 13

It wasn't just about sex.

Dillon stared out his office window the next morning, his thoughts not on town business, but rather on Cassie. He'd thought that he had an intense physical desire for her but it would be, could be, nothing more.

He'd been wrong.

Something had happened to him the day before when he'd covered her body with his own while the shots had rung out. He'd realized at that moment that somehow, someway, his heart had gotten involved. And he didn't like it.

Cassie was nothing like the kind of woman he'd always dreamed of in his life, and even if she was, he and this town weren't what she really wanted.

Throughout the time he'd spent with her, she'd

talked often about her dream of being somebody in New York City. She might be satisfied at the moment selling her paintings through Mary's website, but he feared that wouldn't fulfill her forever.

Even if he managed to talk her into staying here with him, he worried she would eventually come to resent him. As much as he might want her to stay, he refused to be the person who stole her dream from her.

Last night had just been another mistake on his part. He should have never gone into her room the night before. But he would never confess to anyone how utterly terrified he'd been when those shots had occurred.

He hadn't been terrified for his own death, but he'd been afraid that he'd take a bullet that would kill him and then she'd be unprotected and easy prey for the killer.

The evening had fled without him really processing his fear for her, until that moment when he'd stepped into her bedroom supposedly to tell her good-night. And then all he'd needed was to assure himself she was alive and well.

He'd wanted to hear her heart beating reassuringly against his own. He'd needed to feel the warmth of her soft skin against his. He'd been so crazed with his need, he hadn't even thought about protection.

And then, to make matters worse, he'd slept with her in his arms and awakened this morning spooned around her warm, soft body. He'd remained there for several long moments, imagining awakening like that every morning for the rest of his life.

He had to distance himself from her. Dammit, he had to find a way to disengage his emotions, his desire, where she was concerned. It wasn't fair to either of them to keep this going on when they were obviously so wrong for each other.

Painting was Cassie's passion and he wanted to be some woman's passion. He wanted—needed—to be some woman's number one, just as he wanted to make her his number one priority.

Damn, but he needed to get whoever was after Cassie behind bars. The shooting the day before was only a grim reminder that somebody wanted her dead. If only he knew why...then he would be closer to knowing the identity of the guilty.

"Chief?" Annie stuck her head in the door. "Leroy is here to see you."

"Send him in," Dillon replied, grateful for any distraction that would take his thoughts off Cassie and murder.

The old man shuffled in with a grin on his face. "Had to come into town to get Boomer some food," he said as he eased down in the chair opposite Dillon's. "Don't know why I waste my time or money. That old dog isn't happy unless he's eating half of my steak or a couple of hot dogs."

Dillon laughed. "You know people food isn't supposed to be good for a dog."

"That's what they say, but I figure for Boomer

it's now a matter of quality of life versus quantity. He's old enough to have earned his special treats."

"How's everything else going? Did you come in to make a report about something?"

"Nah, this is purely a social call." Leroy leaned back in the chair.

"Want a cup of coffee?" Dillon asked.

"I wouldn't turn up my nose at a cup."

Dillon called to Annie. "Can you bring in two cups of coffee?"

"Sure thing, Chief," she replied.

A few minutes later the two men had their drinks and were talking about old times.

"I always knew you'd wind up being the law in this town. From the time you were four years old you wore a little silver badge and a holster with play guns and said you were going to grow up and lock up all the bad guys."

Dillon smiled. "As I recall you bought me that star and holster for Christmas that year."

"That's the truth," Leroy agreed and then smiled wistfully. "You were the child me and Loretta never had. We had pretty much everything we wanted in life 'cept for children." He took a drink. "When are you going to have some kids of your own? You aren't getting any younger, you know."

"I'm only thirty-five," Dillon protested with a laugh.

"Don't let life pass you right by. You should be building good memories right now. Someday all you'll have left are your memories. They'll be what keep you warm at night and what keep you sane."

"I'm working on it, Leroy," Dillon replied.

"Heard you were staying out at Cassie's. You working on making some memories with her?"

"That arrangement is strictly business," Dillon replied.

Leroy eyed him as if he could see right through Dillon's little white lie. "If you say so. That Cassie is a fine woman."

"Yes, she is," Dillon agreed.

"And pretty, too."

"I get your point, Leroy, but it's complicated."

"Well, then uncomplicate it," the old man replied.

How did you uncomplicate a woman? *If only it was that easy*, Dillon thought.

An hour after Leroy left the office, his words still rang in Dillon's ears. It was time for Dillon to settle down and start building his own family.

Maybe all Cassie was meant to be was his transition woman. She'd made him forget all about Stacy's abandonment. She'd made him realize he might be ready for love again. Maybe it was time he really looked around at all the single women in town.

He was open now to the idea of a wife and children— if he could find the kind of woman he wanted to spend the rest of his life with.

Still, as he thought of all the other available women in Bitterroot, none of them stirred him the way Cassie did. None of them made his breath catch when he saw them. He didn't feel that spark of excitement with anyone but Cassie.

He unlocked the top left drawer of his desk and pulled out the evidence bag that held the ring that had been found in the bottom of the graves.

Despite a lack of evidence, he believed in his gut that this piece of jewelry had fallen off the killer's finger when he'd placed one of the victims in the ground.

It was like Cinderella's glass slipper, only through time Cinderella's foot had widened and the shoe no longer fit. Men's hands got bigger as they grew up, and years of hard work would further change them. There was no way he could try the ring on each of the men's fingers to see if it fit. He had no idea how to find out who the ring had belonged to fifteen years ago.

The only thing he could hope for was that the killer would finally make a mistake that would lead to an arrest. And he hoped he could protect Cassie from whoever wanted her dead.

It was with a vague sense of defeat that he arrived at Cassie's house that evening. She wasn't in the kitchen, but as he entered the house and saw a faint layer of smoke coming from the oven, he knew she'd been down here long enough to put something on to cook.

He opened the oven door and pulled out a pan of blackened meat that he thought might be pork chops. He set the pan on the counter and then climbed the stairs to find Cassie.

She was in her workroom and stood with her back to him and facing her easel. She apparently hadn't heard him come in and he took the opportunity to quietly watch her.

"More green," she murmured and twisted her brush into the paint on her palette. She then dabbed the brush on the canvas where a line of trees had begun to form against a bright blue sky.

Her jeans fit tight on her small, round butt and she wore a long-sleeved blue polo shirt that hugged her small waist.

"No, Cassie, too much," she spoke again, frustration evident in her tone.

A wave of love for her buoyed up inside him, tightening his chest to the point where he couldn't speak. He slowly backed away from the doorway and went back down the stairs.

He opened the refrigerator door and found leftover ham and cheese from the night before. He made them each a sandwich, threw some chips on the plates and grabbed two sodas from the fridge and then carried the plates up the stairs.

She still painted on the picture, obviously completely consumed by the creative vision in her mind. "Dinner is served," he said.

She whirled around, her mouth in a perfect O of surprise and with a streak of blue paint decorating one of her cheeks. "Dillon! You scared the heck out of me." She looked at the plates in his hands and heaved a deep sigh. "The pork chops?"

"Were dead on arrival," he replied.

She motioned for him to set the plates on the worktable and then sighed once again. "I can't stop burning food. This is why I never tried to cook when I was in New York. I just get too distracted to do it right. And I'm not going to apologize again because this is who I am."

It was as if she was intentionally reminding him why she was wrong for him. She pulled a couple of folding chairs out of the closet and he set them up at the table.

He took their sodas off the plates and set them on the tabletop and then they both sat down. "Did something happen today?" he asked. The last time she'd completely blown off dinner was the day she'd found out she'd sold a painting.

"Not really, except Mary and I talked about me going with her to an arts and crafts fair next spring in Oklahoma City. I'd rent a tent next to hers and could show my paintings. It would be like an art show, only not in a gallery but instead in a tent."

"Sounds like a plan. Will you still be here in the spring?" His chest tightened with the question.

Her gaze held his for a long moment and then she looked down at her plate. "I…I don't know."

And therein lay the problem. There was no way he'd put his heart on the line and speak of his love for her not knowing if she'd choose to leave.

He refused to tell another woman he loved her only to watch her drive out of town without a backward glance.

Cassie scratched the end of her nose with the end of her paintbrush and stared critically at her latest painting. It was late Saturday afternoon and she'd been working off and on all day.

If things were different she would have encouraged Dillon to take her to the Watering Hole that evening for a few drinks and some socializing.

That was where all of her men would be tonight. Every Saturday night they all drove into town and blew off steam at the town's popular bar.

She frowned and focused back on her painting. When she'd been in New York she'd painted cityscapes like hundreds of other struggling artists in the Big Apple.

Since moving to the ranch she'd focused solely on ranch and cowboy themes, and she had to admit she'd never painted better than she was right now.

At least she didn't have to worry about making dinner tonight. Dillon was bringing home something from the café. Since the night of the burned pork chops she'd decided the best way to make dinner was to cook it after Dillon got home from work. It made mealtime a little later in the evening, but at least she'd stopped burning things.

Dillon. She released a deep sigh and set her paintbrush down. She grabbed the coffee that she'd poured earlier for herself from the worktable and sank down in one of the folding chairs.

She picked up the sketch she'd made of him after he'd taken her to dinner at the café. She stared at the charcoal image of him and a well of sadness filled her heart.

He'd be home within the hour and they'd spend

another night of avoiding touching, of slightly awkward conversation that was rather superficial. That was how it had been since their last lovemaking bout.

He'd been distant and more quiet than usual. She knew he was retreating from her even as her love for him grew bigger and brighter.

There had been nothing better than seeing his hunger for her in his eyes. There had been nothing more captivating than his gentle kisses after their lovemaking was done. And falling asleep in his strong, warm arms had been pure magic.

But that night had definitely marked a difference in their relationship and she felt now as if she was mourning something she'd never really had.

She mentally shook herself, drank the last of the coffee in her cup and then set the sketch aside and got up to resume her work. If she intended to be here in the spring and did rent a tent next to Mary's, then she wanted to complete at least twelve to fifteen paintings of various sizes through the winter.

She tried to focus on her current painting, but thoughts of Dillon continued to intrude. In the time they had spent together he'd made her feel funny and smart and desirable.

It was funny, but when Dillon looked at her he made her feel like somebody. But what happened when this was all over and he went back to his own life?

Could she see him around town and not feel her heart breaking each time? Could she watch him developing a relationship with another woman and not be affected at all? She didn't know the answer and so she didn't know what her future held.

In any case she wouldn't make her decision to stay or leave based on Dillon. This was probably the most important decision she would ever make in her life and she had to make it based on where she believed she could be happy and fulfilled by herself and in her own soul.

Too distracted to do any more painting, she cleaned up her brushes and paint and then moved downstairs to await his return. She stared out the window where a cold autumn wind had blown all day. The trees were almost bare and winter was just around the corner and still she'd hesitated about leaving here.

If she didn't have Dillon, what was keeping her? All indications from him were that he wouldn't be in her life in any meaningful way in the future, so why hadn't she already called Raymond Humes to make arrangements to sell out? Why wasn't she actively pursuing the dream she'd had for most of her life?

She didn't know the answer and she didn't want to think about it. She didn't want to dwell on thoughts of life without Dillon and she didn't want to think about her future. She just wanted to live in the here and now.

By the time she'd set the table and made a salad to go with whatever he brought in from the café, he was home. He came in with a shopping bag and a tired smile. "Meat loaf and mashed potatoes." He set the bag on the table.

"Sounds good. Why don't you go wash up or whatever and I'll get it on the plates."

"Okay," he agreed.

He left the kitchen and she got busy unloading the containers from the bag and placing the food in serving dishes. She fixed two glasses of ice water and added them to the table and then sat to wait for him.

She had a feeling it was going to be another long night. She'd felt his distance the minute he'd stepped into the house. Over the past two weeks there had been times when she'd actually believed that he might be falling in love with her.

Now she was beginning to believe that what he felt for her was only an intense physical attraction that wasn't followed up with anything deeper than that. It was depressing and a reminder that she'd never been worth much in her entire life.

"Busy day?" she asked him as he came back into the kitchen.

"Not too bad." He joined her at the table.

He'd changed out of his uniform and now wore a pair of jeans and a black pullover polo shirt that hugged his broad shoulders and taut abs. He looked breathtakingly handsome despite the shadows in his eyes.

They helped themselves to the food. "Looks like it has gotten cold out there today," she said.

"That wind is definitely blowing from the north, making the day unusually cold," he agreed. "It feels especially chilly after all the warm days we've had."

"The meat loaf looks good," she said.

"I don't think Daisy and her cooks know how to make anything bad," he replied.

As they ate he told her about people who had come into the police station or who he'd visited with out on the streets. "Abe has Harley picking up trash around town as part of his punishment."

"Good for Abe," she replied.

"Good for Harley and good for the town," he replied.

While they continued to eat he caught her up on all the town news. Daisy had dyed her hair from her signature bright red to a flaming orange for autumn. Steve Kaufman, a widower who spent much of his time reading and drinking coffee at the café, had asked out Jenna McCain, who worked at the general store, although Dillon didn't know if an actual date had taken place yet or not.

"I can't wait until I can get out of this house and go into town and visit with people like a normal person," she said.

"I know this has been hard on you, Cassie," he replied.

"I don't mean to be a whiner."

He laughed. "Cassie, the last thing I would call you would be a whiner."

They were still seated at the table having coffee when darkness fell and a string of headlights appeared coming up the lane from the big garage.

"You always know when it's Saturday night around here," she said. "The men can't wait to spend part of their paychecks on booze and women."

Dillon laughed once again. "It's that way on every ranch in Bitterroot. Saturday night the Watering Hole fills up with every single woman and a bunch of men ready to blow off steam after a week of hard work."

"I just hope somebody manages to get Sawyer home safe and sound." She shook her head. "That man definitely can't hold his liquor."

"At least he's a fairly quiet drunk who just passes out. Zeke Osmond and some of Humes's other ranch hands just get louder and more obnoxious."

"I wish I knew what caused all the bad blood between Raymond and my aunt Cass. I've read almost all of her journals now and I'd hoped to find the answer."

"I'm assuming if you would have found anything pertaining to the crime in those journals you would have told me."

"Absolutely," she replied. "Unfortunately they talk about her decision to staff the ranch with young runaways, but she doesn't mention any of the men by name. I'm on one of the last journals now and according to the date it was written just months before she died. I think there are only a couple more journals left in the shed and I'm assuming they're just like the ones I've already read, mostly filled with her loneliness and grief over my uncle dying and her intense hatred of Raymond."

Once again a visible weariness crept across his features. "Why don't you go sit and relax in the living room and I'll clean up the kitchen," she said.

Normally he would have protested and insisted

he help, but tonight he simply murmured a thanks and left the kitchen. Cassie cleared the plates and glasses and put the leftovers in the refrigerator and then moved to the great room where Dillon sat in the chair.

"Want to watch something?" she asked and gestured toward the television.

"Sure."

She took the remote from the coffee table and turned on the television, grateful for the noise it provided. The awkwardness was back between them and she didn't know what to do about it.

"Do you want it on another channel?" she asked.

"No, this is fine…unless you want to watch something else?"

"This is fine with me," she replied. The stilted pleasantness between them made her want to scream. The hours just before bedtime had become particularly excruciating.

She thought of the gun upstairs in her nightstand drawer. She knew how to aim and pull the trigger. Maybe that and the alarm system was all she needed to protect herself from whoever was after her.

Maybe it was finally time to let Dillon off the hook and send him home. Her heart squeezed tight at the very thought of him not being in this house with her. She'd grown so accustomed to his presence here. And she had to admit there was more than a little fear involved in facing being alone in the house.

But he looked so miserable, and there was no question that things had gotten tense between them since they had made love again, and she didn't know how to fix it.

She could love him all she wanted, but she would never be the kind of woman he was looking for in his life. She would never be the little homemaker he wanted. Maybe she had to love him enough to let him go.

A touch of fear tightened her chest as she thought once again of being all alone here and facing a potential killer. Surely with the alarm and the gun she'd be okay.

"Dillon?"

He turned to look at her and his eyes were dark and unreadable. "Yes?"

"Maybe it's time we stop all this."

"Stop all what?" A confused wrinkle appeared across his forehead.

"We both know you can't stay here forever. I have the security system and a gun. Surely I'd be okay here alone."

He looked at her as if she'd grown a second head. "Cassie, those few minutes we spent shooting in no way made me comfortable about your ability to use a gun. Are you trying to get rid of me?"

"I have the feeling that lately you'd be glad to be rid of me," she confessed. "You have to know things have gotten kind of weird between us, Dillon."

"Yeah, they have," he agreed. He leaned back in the chair and swiped a hand down his jaw. His gaze held hers for several long moments. "I'll tell you what the problem is. We both know we're wrong for each other. You have some childhood dream to pursue and there's no way I want to be the man to steal that dream from you. I just hope you find whatever it is you need to find back in New York."

"And I hope you find the kind of woman you want, although I have my doubts."

He raised an eyebrow. "And why is that?"

She was suddenly irritated with him. "Your childhood dream of the little woman waiting breathlessly for you to come home from work while filling the kitchen with the scents of cookies baking is more than a little antiquated."

"We both know you'll never be that woman," he replied curtly.

"I don't want to be that woman," she said tersely. "Someday I want to be a wife and mother, but I also want to be more than that."

"Right, you want to be famous. It isn't enough for you just to be Cassie. You are still looking to somehow get acceptance from your parents. Face it, Cassie, you're clinging to some pretty heavy baggage in your own life. The only person you really have to please is yourself."

"I was never good enough just being me," she retorted.

"So, you think your happiness is in some big city trying to be somebody important." His tone had become irritable, as well.

"I don't know where my happiness is," she replied. In the back of her mind she was wondering how this crazy, slightly painful conversation was going to end.

Dillon got out of his chair. "That's the real problem with you, Cassie. You don't realize that your happiness comes from inside you." The ring of his cell phone interrupted them. "Chief Bowie," he said into the phone.

He listened and frowned. "I'll be right there." He hung up the phone. "I've got to go," he said to her.

"What's happened?" she asked.

"There's been a wreck…apparently a bad one and Leroy was involved. He's been taken to the emergency room at the hospital and he's asking for me."

"Oh, no." She quickly rose from the sofa. The conversation they'd just had faded from her mind as she saw the deep concern on Dillon's face. She knew Leroy had been like a second father to him when he'd been growing up.

She followed Dillon into the kitchen where he grabbed his coat off a hook next to the back door and shrugged it on. He then disarmed the alarm and turned back to her. "I'll be back as soon as I can."

"You take all the time you need and I'll say a prayer for Leroy."

His gaze burned into hers and he reached up and dragged a finger down her cheek. "You know why things have gotten so weird between us? It's because I've fallen in love with you, Cassie. And I don't like it. I don't like it one bit." Without waiting for any reply, he flew out the door and into the darkness of the night.

She reset the alarm and then moved to the window to watch his car drive out of sight. He loved her. Her heart sang and a fluttering warmth enveloped her. He loved her!

The song in her heart only lasted for a single refrain and then clunked to a discordant ending. But he'd also said she wasn't the kind of woman he wanted in his life. He'd told her that they were all wrong for each other. He'd said that he loved her and he didn't like it.

No matter how much she loved him she couldn't compromise who she was at her core to be the little lady he wanted in his life. Who knew, maybe he could eventually find that kind of woman, but it would never be her.

She left the kitchen and went up the stairs. Maybe it was a good time to finally clean out that shelf in her closet, and while she worked she needed to do some soul-searching to come to a real decision about whether she wanted to throw Dillon's love and Bitterroot to the wind and go back to the city, or stay here and hope that somehow, someway, Dillon would see that they might be very right for each other.

Chapter 14

Dillon drove fast, with his lights swirling and his siren blaring as he headed back into town. He couldn't believe he'd told Cassie he was in love with her. But he refused to think about that now. He had to get to the hospital and check on Leroy.

Brenda hadn't had any real details about the accident, so he had no idea how serious Leroy's injuries might be. He also didn't know how or where the accident had occurred. All he did know was that he was worried sick about Leroy.

He slowed as he approached the Bitterroot Hospital. Although small, the hospital boasted exceptional doctors and updated equipment, but if Leroy's injuries were bad enough he'd have to be transported to one of the bigger hospitals in Oklahoma City.

The first person he saw when he entered the emergency waiting room was Deputy Ben Taylor. "Ben, how's Leroy?"

"He's pretty banged up. He's in X-ray right now, but before they took him back he was asking for you."

"How and where did this happen?" The two men walked over to the dark green plastic chairs and sat side by side.

"On Main Street at the light just north of the Watering Hole. Ace Sanders ran the light and smashed right into the side of Leroy's truck. I arrested Ace on scene and he was taken to the jail."

"Drunk?" Dillon asked.

"As a skunk," Ben replied. "But the wreck sobered him up quick enough and now he's beside himself worrying about Leroy."

"What in the hell was Leroy doing driving around after dark on a Saturday night?"

"He told me Boomer needed some hot dogs."

Dillon leaned back in the chair and released a deep sigh. Ace Sanders was one of Humes's men, and Dillon knew Raymond would have him bailed out first thing Monday morning. He just hoped Leroy fared as well.

"Does Ace have insurance?" he asked.

"Yes, and it's a good thing. Leroy's truck was crushed in. Thank God it was on the passenger side, but he wasn't wearing his seat belt so he got tossed around pretty good. The truck is still drivable. Mike drove it here so that Leroy would have a way to get home when they release him."

Dillon sighed again, this time in frustration. "I never understand why people don't wear their damned seat belts when it's proven they save lives. I just hope he isn't badly hurt. What are they X-raying?"

"His ribs and his skull. He banged his head against the side window and he was complaining of some chest pain."

The two men fell silent as the minutes ticked by. As Dillon waited to see Leroy, his thoughts returned to Cassie. Were his ideas about a future wife antiquated? Was it possible he was clinging to an old dream that had no real place in the world today?

He was probably all kinds of a fool to have allowed those words of love to slip out of his mouth. Now things would really be awkward between them.

Still, there was no way in hell he was leaving her at that ranch alone with only a security system and a gun she wasn't proficient with standing between her and a killer.

The murderer had to be getting desperate. He'd made two failed attempts in a relatively short period of time. His frustration level had to be off the charts. And hopefully that would make him make a mistake.

"What's taking so long?" Dillon asked, once again worried about Leroy.

"You should know time always moves slowly in the emergency room," Ben said.

Finally, the doors to the ER opened and Dr. Eric

Washington walked over to where Dillon and Ben sat. The two quickly got to their feet.

"How is he?" Dillon asked.

"He's been better, but I don't see anything on the X-rays to cause any real concern. He's going to feel like he's been run over by a truck for a few days, and he has some cuts and contusions, but he's going to survive."

"Thank God," Dillon replied as a wave of huge relief swept through him. Leroy might drive him a little crazy with his reports of aliens, but the old man had a special place in Dillon's heart.

"Despite his protests I'm going to keep him overnight for observation, and we'll see about letting him go sometime later tomorrow afternoon. But in the meantime he's been asking for you," Eric said to Dillon.

"I'll just head back out. You know how it is on Saturday nights…plenty of fools on the road," Ben said.

"Thanks, Ben," Dillon replied. "I appreciate you being here with Leroy."

Ben nodded and left. Dillon then followed Eric through the ER doors. He heard Leroy before he saw him. "I can't stay here overnight. You've got to let me out of here. I got hot dogs to get home to Boomer," Leroy exclaimed loudly. "I can't stay here."

Dillon opened the curtain Eric gestured to and saw Leroy in the bed and Vanessa Duncan taking his blood pressure. Leroy sported a huge bruise on the side of his face. "Don't get yourself all worked up, Mr. Atkinson," Vanessa said. "It isn't good for you."

"Listen to Vanessa and behave yourself," Dillon said.

"Dillon, I'm glad you're here." Leroy sat up in the bed as Vanessa removed the blood pressure cuff.

"I'll just leave you two alone," Vanessa said and left the room, trailing the scent of a spicy perfume behind her.

"You know I'm about to yell at you," Dillon said.

Leroy looked at him in surprise. "For what? I didn't do anything wrong. That darned Ace Sanders ran the red light and crashed right into me."

"And where was your seat belt? If you'd had it on maybe you wouldn't have that big bruise on the side of your face and wouldn't be feeling like crap right now. I should give you a damned ticket for not wearing it."

Leroy appeared chagrined. "I'm sorry. I promise I'll have it strangling me from now on whenever I drive. But that's not what I'm worried about now. I'm worried about Boomer. He's used to getting a hot dog every night before I go to bed. If they're going to keep me here overnight then Boomer is going to be so upset. Unless..."

"Unless what?" Dillon asked warily.

"Maybe you could get the hot dogs out of my truck and swing by my place and make sure he has enough water and he gets his treat before bedtime. Please, Dillon. You know that old dog is all I got."

Dillon doubted that Boomer would have a breakdown if he didn't get a hot dog tonight, but he feared Leroy might go off the deep end if he denied this request.

"Okay, I'll go take care of Boomer and you stay here and take care of yourself," Dillon replied.

Leroy shot him a look of relief. "You always were a good boy, Dillon. And you've grown up to be everything all of us wanted you to be."

An unexpected well of emotion rose up in Dillon's chest. "You and Loretta were always good to me, Leroy. Don't you worry about Boomer. I'll see that he gets his hot dog tonight and hopefully you'll be out of here and back at home sometime tomorrow. Now, don't give everyone a hard time here, and I'll check in with you tomorrow, okay?"

Minutes later Dillon strode across the parking lot to Leroy's truck. His stomach clenched as he saw the damage on the passenger side. Leroy had been very lucky not to have sustained more serious injuries.

He found the hot dogs in a shopping bag on the passenger floor and then headed out to Leroy's place. His thoughts were instantly filled with Cassie. He called her.

She answered on the second ring, her voice half breathless. "Everything okay there?" he asked with immediate concern.

"It's fine," she assured him. "I'm in the middle of cleaning out the shelf in my closet. I now have an empty shelf and tons of junk in the middle of my bedroom floor. How's Leroy doing?"

"A little battered and bruised, but he'll be okay."

"That's good to hear. I'm sure you're relieved."

"I am," he admitted. "When I got to the hospital I was assuming the worst."

He explained to her that he was on his way to Leroy's house to see about the dog. "It shouldn't be too long and then I'll be back to your place."

"Okay, and then I think we need to have a talk," she replied. There was nothing in her tone to indicate what was going on in her head. Was she going to insist he move out? Was she going to tell him she'd decided to sell out?

"All right," he replied. "I'll see you in a little while."

He ended the call and his stomach churned with uncertainty. It was at that moment he realized he wanted Cassie to be the woman in his future. The dream he'd once had for himself was nothing but a stupid fantasy and it was time to let it go and embrace the woman who already owned his heart.

There was just one small problem. He'd told her he loved her and now the ball was in her court, and he had no idea if he'd be enough for her.

Cassie eyed the mess on her floor and was almost sorry she'd begun the project to start with. Blankets, boxes of shoes and old framed pictures battled for space on the floor with faded artificial flowers, spare bed pillows and sundry other items.

She hadn't really looked at anything as she'd taken it off the shelf, but she intended to weed through the items and put them away in a more orderly fashion.

Of course it didn't help that she kept getting distracted by Dillon's words right before he'd left the house. *I've fallen in love with you, Cassie. And I don't like it.*

Over and over again the words played in her mind, filling her first with a sweet euphoria and then a wave of utter confusion. She was an artist. Artists visualized things, but there was no way she could visualize what her future held. If he didn't like being in love with her and clung to some fantasy of the perfect woman for him, then there was no happy ending for her here with him.

But she'd also begun to understand that maybe New York City didn't hold her happy ending, either. She had spent her whole life trying to fill a hole that had been left there by her parents. But now she recognized that nothing she would do in her life would magically change the cold, distant people who had raised her.

She walked into the bathroom with a clean nightgown and stared for a moment into the mirror above the sink. "You will never be a famous artist," she said to her reflection.

Funny, it didn't hurt to believe those words. In fact, if she was honest with herself she'd admit that she'd known that particular truth for a very long time. Otherwise she would have never left New York when she'd inherited the ranch. She would have had the lawyer take care of selling it.

Dillon was right. If she was going to heal that hole inside her, it wasn't by living in a specific place or pleasing a specific person. She needed to find the worth and love within herself.

She took off her clothes and pulled on the nightgown. She couldn't wait until Dillon got home so they could talk, so she could tell him she was in love with him, too. She had no idea if him knowing that she loved him would change anything, but she had to share with him what was in her heart.

In the meantime she had a mess to clean up. She grabbed the two spare bed pillows and walked into the hallway. She quickly placed two fresh pillowcases on them and then carried them into the room where Dillon stayed to put them on the empty shelf in that closet.

Once that was done, she stood in the room and just breathed in the scent of him. She'd been hot for him for months, but the truth was, while she was still intensely drawn to him physically, her love for him was so much more than that.

He'd captivated her with his laughter, and challenged her with his mind. The fact that he was going to a house to feed a dog a hot dog only shone the light on what a good and kind man he was.

He was everything she'd never really imagined. She'd never known she was capable of loving a man as much as she loved Dillon.

She left the bedroom and returned to the mess on her floor. The artificial flowers found a new home in the bottom of a trash bag, as did several broken umbrellas. Her aunt Cass had been something of a pack rat and apparently had a reluctance to throw things away even after they'd outlived their usefulness.

Finally she sank down on the floor to address all of the old framed photos she'd taken off the wall when she'd first arrived months before. She'd replaced them with some of her cityscape paintings on the wall. They were the paintings that had never sold because she was a good artist, but she'd never be a great artist.

This little epiphany didn't break her heart; she knew it was simply the truth. Dillon was right. She'd been holding on to a little girl's dream of being famous and now it was time to let that go and just be Cassie.

The first photo she picked up was one of her aunt Cass and uncle Hank. They were locked in an embrace and happiness shone from both of their faces. She touched the face of the woman who had left her the ranch.

From what everyone had told her, Cass had been a tough but caring woman. She had to have been strong to take on twelve young runaways who had difficult backgrounds and basically raise them into good men.

Cassie only hoped one day she could be as strong and as loving as her aunt Cass had been.

She set the picture aside and grabbed another one. This one was of her aunt on horseback with a bullwhip in her hand. Cass's acumen with the bullwhip was legendary. Cassie had heard her aunt could take the eye out of a snake with one flick of that whip.

The next picture made her instantly smile. Twelve teenagers lined up like a most-wanted photo from the Old West. Cowboy hats sat on their heads and they were clad in T-shirts and jeans. They all looked achingly young, but it was easy to identify Sawyer in the group. He stood taller than most of the men, with his slightly curly, coppery hair.

It was also easy to pick out Clay, with his blond hair and sparkling blue eyes. One by one she put young faces with names. They were all there, all of the men who had worked for her aunt and who now worked for her. Maybe she should rehang these pictures on the wall and take down her paintings. These men and this place were now in her heart and soul.

She put the photo aside and picked up one that was just Cass and a young, handsome Adam. Adam must have been about fifteen when the photo had been taken.

Her heart stuttered to a stop. The ring that Dillon had told her about…the ring he believed belonged to the killer. It was on his finger. She looked closer, wondering if she was seeing things. No, it was there…a gold ring with a black onyx stone.

Oh, God…it was Adam. Adam was the killer. He wore the damning ring that had wound up in a grave of murdered boys. How else would the ring have found its way into the bottom of a grave?

She didn't know how long she sat staring at the photo as chills raced up and down her spine. Had Adam locked her into the shed and then rescued her to take any suspicion off himself?

It was hard to believe he'd been the one who had broken into the house and swung an ax into the walls as he'd come up the stairs, terrorizing her before he intended to kill her.

She stood on shaky legs and with a heart that raced. Adam. His name rang in her head with a deadly clang. Why had he killed those boys? And why did he now want to kill her?

Since she'd arrived here he'd been so patient and kind to her, and she had responded with friendliness and care. So, what had gone wrong?

A loud knock sounded from downstairs, pulling her from her horrified reverie. She grabbed her cell phone off the nightstand and went down the stairs, hoping it was Dillon and he couldn't see the keypad in the dark to let himself in.

It wasn't Dillon. It was Adam. Oh, God, she'd thought he'd gone into town with the other men. He was probably here to give her the nightly ranch report. She couldn't let him inside. She needed to get rid of him. She desperately needed to call Dillon and tell him what she'd discovered.

Adam smiled at her through the window, wearing the same pleasant expression he always wore when she was around him. But it was a lie. That smile… that handsome face was only a facade of pure evil.

Her heart thundered. She couldn't let him see her fear, her utter revulsion. She had to appear perfectly normal. Sick. It definitely wouldn't be hard to fake that she was sick to her stomach.

She shut off the alarm and then raised the window next to the door an inch. "Adam, I'm really not feeling well right now. Can you check in with me tomorrow night?"

"Sure," he replied easily and then frowned. "Is there anything you need that you don't have in the house?"

"No, it's just a bit of an upset stomach. I'm actually on my way to bed."

"Okay, Cassie. I hope you feel better," he replied.

"Thanks, I'll talk to you tomorrow." She closed the window and relocked it, set the alarm and then turned to go back up the stairs, eager to call Dillon to let him know about the picture she'd found.

She was on the second stair when a loud crash came from the kitchen and the alarm began to shrill a warning. She screamed and raced up the stairs as another crash resounded. And another…and another. The sound of splintering wood galvanized her into action.

"Cassie!" Adam yelled, letting her know he was inside the house.

She reached the top of the stairs, and instead of running to her bedroom, she ducked into the room where Dillon slept. Frantic with fear, she slid under the bed and dialed Dillon's number.

He answered and she didn't speak a word, afraid that Adam would hear her voice. She simply hoped Dillon heard the scream of the alarm and would know she was in trouble.

"Cassie, it's time to die!" Adam's voice was horrifyingly close, and she turned her phone off so he wouldn't hear Dillon's response and discover her hiding place.

Still, she knew there was no way Dillon would be able to get here in time to save her. She was on her own with a man who wanted to kill her, and her gun might as well be a million miles away.

The sound of slow, deliberate footsteps coming up the stairs tightened her breath painfully in her chest. Beneath the low-hanging bedspread she peeked out and saw his boots just outside the room.

She squeezed her eyes closed and pressed her lips tightly together and prayed for him to walk on by. For what seemed like an agonizing amount of time he remained standing in place as silent, frantic tears chased each other down her cheeks.

Finally he went straight down the hallway to her bedroom, and she quickly slid out from beneath the bed and ran down the stairs. The upstairs of the house would be a death trap with no means of escape.

"Cassie!" She heard his voice above the din of the ringing alarm and knew he was coming after her.

She ran through the great room and into the kitchen. She exploded out of the broken back door and into the cold night. She had no plan, but fled into the darkness with sheer panic.

Chapter 15

Boomer was happily wagging his tail as Dillon fed him not one, but two hot dogs. He'd already let the dog outside to do his business and had filled his water bowl.

He planned on coming by first thing in the morning to let the old pooch out once again. Hopefully, by sometime in the afternoon. Leroy would be back home again.

Just as it had been the last time Dillon had been inside the house, the windows were all covered with sheets of aluminum foil and the walls were filled with framed pictures.

Most of the pictures were of Loretta and Leroy... a testimony to the fact that love lived on even after death. There were also photos of Dillon's mother and father and an embarrassing number of Dillon as a young boy.

Yes, Leroy had loved and he'd loved well, and the memory of that love was what warmed Leroy's life now. And in the end wasn't that all that really mattered?

He'd just placed the rest of the hot dogs in the refrigerator when his phone rang. He saw Cassie's number and answered.

He instantly pulled the phone from his ear as a shrill scream resounded from the device. "Cassie?" he yelled. She didn't reply but the sound of the alarm was enough to move him into action.

He left Leroy's house with his heart thundering in fear. If the alarm was ringing then somebody had breached the security. Dammit, the killer had obviously known she was alone in the house and had taken the opportunity to strike.

He got into his car and gunned the engine to life, then with lights swirling and siren screaming he took off. Gravel and dust spit up as he stepped on the gas, every muscle in his body rigid and a knot of tension tight in his chest.

Despite his speed there was no way he could get to the Holiday ranch fast enough. He tightened his fingers on the steering wheel as his heart beat a frantic rhythm in his chest.

He tried to call her again, but it rang and rang. She didn't pick up and it kept going to voice mail. Oh, God, why didn't she answer? What was happening right now? Was it already too late? Was he already too late?

Why hadn't he thought more carefully about leaving her all alone? Because he'd gotten sloppy. He'd just assumed with the security system nobody would attempt to break in again. He'd once again underestimated his foe.

Visions of Sam Kelly swam in his head, along with a picture of seven skeletons. A faint nausea rose up in the back of his throat as he thought of Cassie in the house with the man who had killed all those people.

He couldn't drive any faster and he couldn't magically transport himself to get to her. Dammit, this was all his fault.

He hated that it was possible the last words she heard from him was that he loved her and he didn't like it. He did like it and he wanted to continue loving Cassie for as long as she wanted him to.

He had to get there in time. She had to be okay. He had to believe that he would get there before something terrible happened to her.

The night was unusually dark, with the moon hidden beneath thick clouds. Thankfully, he met no other cars on the road, for he was flying at a high rate of speed and he didn't want anything to slow him down.

Finally, he turned into the ranch's long drive and skidded to a stop at the back door...the door that hung in chopped pieces. Once again nausea churned in his stomach. He quickly punched in the code to halt the alarm from ringing.

He pulled his gun and stepped into the house. An ominous silence greeted him. Was he already too late? Had the killer already committed his act of madness and fled?

His chest ached in a way it had never hurt before. He gripped his gun firmly, unsure what he might find. "Cassie!" he yelled loudly and then waited for a response. There was none…not a gasp, not a whimper… nothing.

He checked the downstairs, only slightly grateful he saw nothing that would indicate a struggle had taken place. Slowly he climbed the stairs, dread filling his heart.

Whirling into the bedroom where he slept, his breath whooshed out of him as he saw nothing amiss. But his relief lasted only a minute as he spied Cassie's cell phone under one of the twin beds. He was afraid to speculate on how it had gotten there.

He slowly moved down the hall and stepped into the spare bedroom. Nothing in here, either. His heart was beating so fast, so frantically, he could hear it inside his head. Nothing in the bathroom or in her workroom.

There was only her bedroom left to check. His gun hand trembled slightly as he gripped the gun tightly. Despite the coolness of the house, a bead of sweat worked its way down the side of his face.

He was terrified he'd find her in bed, the back of

her skull split open. He was petrified that he'd find her body stuffed in her closet.

He stepped into the room and only breathed a sigh of relief after he checked the adjoining bathroom and the closet. She wasn't here. She was noplace inside the house.

He flew back down the stairs and to the back door. He stared out into the darkness, where the silhouettes of the outbuildings were visible.

Was it possible somehow she had managed to get out of the house and had run to one of the outbuildings to hide? Or had the killer taken her somewhere and her disappearance would just be another mystery related to this cursed ranch?

Cassie ran as fast as she could when she left the house. She didn't even feel the rough ground beneath her bare feet or the cold night air. Her brain was in a fog of terror, making it difficult to know where to go or where to hide.

She gasped with her exertion, crying out as she tripped and fell to the ground. Her knee hit something sharp and as she scrambled to her feet pain battled with her fear.

She was vaguely aware of the warmth of blood sliding down her leg from her knee. She shot a glance over her shoulder. Adam was in sight, stalking her with an ax swinging in front of him. Any pain she might have felt was usurped by the sheer terror that rushed through her.

For a moment she thought about running to the

cowboy motel and knocking on the doors. Maybe one of the men had stayed behind when they'd all left for town.

But there wasn't time, and it wasn't a gamble she was willing to take. Surely if anyone was in one of the rooms they'd be able to hear the scream of the alarm coming from the house.

Instead of running toward the cowboy motel, she headed for the barn. Her only hope was to hide somewhere and hope that Dillon got home quickly.

She ducked inside, where the darkness was profound. She had no idea if she'd made a mistake or not, but there was no time to change her mind.

All she wanted was a corner to hide in, a place where Adam wouldn't find her until Dillon could get here. And she prayed Dillon had answered her call, heard the alarm and knew she was in danger.

She bumped around in the darkness and tried to visualize the barn interior in her mind. Adam's office was to the right and that was the last place she wanted to die.

There on the left, hay bales were stacked high and deep. Maybe she could burrow down in the hay and be safe. She could no longer hear the house siren ringing. In fact, there was nothing surrounding her but a silence broken only by her ragged breathing.

"Cassie," Adam's voice boomed from the barn door.

She stuck her fist in her mouth to staunch the sound of her breaths. She had to be quiet as a mouse, otherwise he would know where she was and she wouldn't survive this night.

"I'm sorry, Cassie, but it has to end this way." He slammed the ax into something and every muscle in her body jumped. This was a nightmare and there was no hope of waking up and being safe.

"You were mine. We were meant to be together, but you betrayed me." The sentence was once again punctuated with another whack of the ax.

What was he talking about? He was obviously delusional. She'd never given him any indication that she was interested in him romantically. But it didn't matter what was reality. All that mattered was *his* reality.

"Whores have to die, Cassie. I learned that from my mama. She was one and I took care of her. From the time I was just a baby until I strangled her to death she'd take me with her to meet her lovers and leave me in the car while she had sex in cheap motel rooms. I killed her when I was fourteen and buried her body in the woods. Everyone thought she'd run away with one of her many lovers."

A new horror swept through Cassie. He'd killed his own mother? Oh, God, why hadn't she seen the evil inside him before now? How had he fooled her so completely?

"I've only loved one woman before you, Cassie, and that was your aunt. She was an angel and that's why I had to kill all those boys. She was giving them all a chance at a new life, but they were nothing but losers who didn't have her best interests at heart."

His voice came from the opposite side of the barn and she nearly gasped when she saw a beam of light. The darkness had been her friend, but with a flashlight he would eventually be able to find her.

"One of them was a thief. I cut off his head and his fingers. Three of them were dopeheads so they had to go. And the last three were just looking for a free ride and didn't want to work, so they weren't what Cass needed."

His voice was closer now and she fought her need to scream. She wanted to bury herself deeper in the hay, but she was afraid if she tried he'd hear her rustling around.

"When Cass died I thought my life was over, but then you arrived and I knew it was destined that we marry and run this place together. I was your protector, Cassie. I killed Sam Kelly for you. He said something very crude about wanting to get you naked and alone in the hay."

A new sob threatened to spill out of her. Sam had been killed because of her. And now she was going to die, as well, and the secret of all the dead people would die with her.

The flashlight beam hit her in the face, blinding her. "There you are," Adam exclaimed triumphantly. She skittered backward in an attempt to escape him.

He grabbed one of her ankles and yanked her toward him. Finally, as he dragged her across the barn floor, she released the scream that had been trapped inside her since the moment he'd broken into her home.

* * *

Dillon had just checked the stables and called for backup when he heard Cassie's scream. A wild elation battled with a horrifying panic. She was alive... but in deep trouble. The barn. The scream had come from the barn.

He ran across the ground faster than he'd ever run before. The elation of knowing she was alive lasted only a second, but it was fear for her that fueled him forward.

Gripping a flashlight in one hand and his gun in the other, his heartbeat raced painfully fast. He had to get to her in time. She couldn't be another statistic on his desk.

He flew into the entrance of the barn and froze at the sight of Adam dragging Cassie across the floor, his ax held in his hand.

"Adam!" he cried.

The man turned to look at him and smiled, and then hefted the ax high above his head. Cassie screamed and Dillon fired his gun.

The bullet hit Adam dead center in his chest. Still he held the ax in a position of attack. Dillon fired once again. This shot took him down and the ax clattered to the floor next to him. Adam didn't move.

Dillon kicked the ax across the floor and then raced over to Cassie, who was curled up in a fetal ball and sobbing uncontrollably. "Cassie, it's okay. You're safe now." He crouched down beside her. He aimed his flashlight beam first at her pale white face and frightened eyes. As he scanned downward the sight of blood pooling from a jagged cut in her knee jarred him.

"Cassie...you're hurt. We need to get you to the hospital." Dillon's stomach churned. "Did Adam hit you with the ax?"

She shook her head. "No... I fell... I was trying to get away... He was after me." The words came between sobs. "He killed them, Dillon...he killed them all."

Sirens sounded from the distance, coming closer and closer. It felt like it had been hours since he'd called for backup. Yet, everything had happened so fast.

"Come on, Cassie. Let's get you out of here." He helped her to her feet and she cried out in pain as she tried to put weight on her bloody leg.

Dillon swooped her up in his arms and carried her out of the barn. "Ben," he called to the uniformed man running toward them. "Adam Benson is in the barn. Make sure he's dead and take care of things here. I'm taking Cassie to the hospital."

"Cassie, are you okay?" Ben asked.

"I'll be fine." She began to shiver and hid her face in the crook of Dillon's neck. The warmth of her breath against him filled him with a deep contentment. She was alive. Thank God she was wonderfully alive.

She clung to him as he carried her to his car. Although he was curious as to what Adam might have said to her, he didn't want to ask her any questions until she was ready to talk. She had been through a horrifying trauma. He might be the chief of police, but at the moment he was just a man tending to his woman.

He gently placed her into the passenger seat and took off his jacket and wrapped it around her. He then ripped off his shirt and told her to hold it to her still-bleeding knee. He hurried around to the driver's side of the car and got in.

As they pulled out onto the road into town he turned on the car heater. She had to be freezing, clad only in his jacket and the short silk nightgown. At least she'd stopped crying, but she was unnaturally pale and quiet.

He couldn't begin to imagine what she'd been through. He also had no idea how traumatized she was right now. He just wanted to get her to the hospital as quickly as possible and let a doctor determine what her condition was at the moment.

"I thought I was dead." Her voice was a soft whisper. "I thought for sure you were going to find my dead body and my death would just be another mystery that people would talk about for years to come." She began to weep quietly once again.

"It's over, Cassie. You've been so brave through all of this and now it's really over. Adam will never be able to hurt anyone ever again."

She swiped at her tears. "He told me he killed his mother when he was fourteen and buried her body in the woods. He also killed Sam Kelly because Sam said something crude about me. How did he manage to hide his craziness for so long? Why didn't any of the other men or anyone else see that he was a monster? Why didn't I see it?"

"I don't know. I certainly didn't see it," he confessed. There were so many things he wanted to say to her, but now wasn't the time or the place.

By the time they reached the hospital she'd told him about the picture she'd found with Adam wearing the ring and how she had pretended to be sick when he'd come to the back door to give her his daily report.

"You can tell me more once the doctor sees you," he said as he parked the car in front of the emergency room. Minutes later she was being wheeled back into a room and Dillon was cooling his heels in the waiting room.

He sank down in a chair and slumped back, for the first time really processing what had happened. If he'd been one minute longer in getting to the barn, he knew with certainty Adam would have killed Cassie.

He could have lost her. Tears welled up in his eyes and blurred his vision. *You could still lose her*, a little voice whispered in his head.

This whole harrowing incident would probably make it much easier on her to decide to sell out and head back to the city. This place would only be terrible memories for her. As much as he wanted her here forever, he would have to let her go if that was her wish.

Still, at least she was safe. Through the grace of God, he had gotten to her in time. He swiped the tears from his eyes. There would be lots of work ahead of him to close this case down. Thankfully, he knew his men would be working to process the scene both inside the barn and in the house.

Finally the voices of the seven dead young men would be silenced. Adam's death had been their justice and now Dillon's peace.

He had no idea how much time had passed when Dr. Clayton Rivers finally came out to speak to him. Dillon scrambled to his feet. "How is she?"

"She's got some cuts and contusions and I put twelve stiches in her knee, but that was the worst of her injuries. She couldn't tell me what she fell on so I also gave her a tetanus shot just to be safe."

"How's she doing mentally?" Dillon asked.

Clayton's brown eyes deepened in hue. "She's doing better now. She was definitely shaken up when you brought her in. We've moved her to a room for the night and she's been sedated."

"Can I see her?" Even if she was sleeping Dillon needed to see her again before he headed back to the ranch to deal with his investigation. He needed to assure himself she was really okay before he closed his eyes to sleep later.

"As long as you make it brief," Clayton replied. "I don't need to tell you that she's been through a traumatic experience and what she needs right now more than anything is rest."

"I'll just be a few minutes," Dillon replied.

"She's in room 103."

"Thanks, Clayton." Dillon turned and headed down the corridor that would take him to her room.

The hospital was quiet and the lights in the hallway were dimmed. Dillon looked at his watch and was vaguely surprised to realize it was after one.

He turned into her room and his heart squeezed tight. She looked so small and so fragile in the bed. A small light was on above her bed and her blond curls looked achingly soft.

She appeared to be sound asleep. He remained standing just inside the doorway, drinking in the sight of her. Thank God she was in the hospital and not in the morgue. His chest hurt as he thought of all that might have happened to her.

Before he could back out of the room her eyes opened and a soft smile curved her lips. "Dillon."

He walked over to the chair next to her bed and sat. "Cassie, how are you feeling?"

"Wonderful," she replied drowsily. "They gave me something in my IV and I'm simply wonderful."

Jeez, he was so crazy about this woman. "I'm glad you aren't hurting. I'm glad you're okay." The words were so inadequate to express the relief…the love that burned in his heart.

"You're my hero, Dillon. You saved my life. If you hadn't come when you had, he would have killed me." Her eyes darkened for a moment and he reached out and took her hand in his. Her hand was wonderfully warm in his.

"But I got there in time and you were smart to

get out of the house and run. You were smart and so brave, Cassie."

"If I could have gotten to my gun I would have shot him through his evil heart…or I might have possibly shot myself by accident." She offered him a wry grin even as her eyes began to drift closed. "I think we need to work some more on my shooting abilities…"

She was out. He remained seated for several long minutes just watching her sleep. The sound of her steady, faint breathing was music to his ears.

Had she been joking when she'd said they needed to work on her gun skills? If she was serious, did that mean she intended to stick around?

He hoped so. He wanted her with him in Bitterroot for the rest of his life. He desperately wanted to be enough for her… He wanted to be her happiness.

He finally let go of her hand, got up and walked quietly out of her room and then on out to his car. He needed to get back out to the ranch and see how things were going there.

When he reached the ranch he went into the house, where Ben told him the medical examiner had already come and taken away Adam's body. Photos had been taken and the ax had been placed in evidence. "We didn't have a key to his room and wasn't sure you'd want us to break in," Ben explained. "So, we haven't done anything in there yet."

"I know where Cassie keeps the keys." Dillon opened the drawer in the desk and plucked out the large key ring with the glittery charm. "I'll check it out while you all finish up in here."

He left the house and walked toward the cowboy motel. The cowboys had all returned from their night of revelry and now stood in a somber group near their rooms.

They all descended on him as he got closer. Questions flew from them, most of them inquiries about Cassie. He assured them she was fine and in the hospital for the night but should be returning home tomorrow.

"We still can't believe it was Adam," Brody said.

"And why in the hell did he go after Cassie?" Clay added.

Another volley of questions shot off, these expressing their shock that their foreman, their brother, was the killer. Dillon held up his hands to still them.

"I don't have all the answers right now. Cassie was in no condition for me to question tonight. I'll know more tomorrow." Dillon frowned. "Where's Sawyer?"

"In bed. We almost always have to carry him home and tuck him in after he's had a few beers," Flint explained. "We all still can't believe it was Adam."

"But we've all talked and understand now that Adam was here before all of us," Clay added. "He's responsible for those seven skeletons, isn't he?"

Dillon nodded. "All of you go get some sleep. Cassie is going to need all of your support through the coming days. I'll try to answer any questions you might have more thoroughly tomorrow."

He waited until all of them had disappeared into their rooms and then he unlocked Adam's door, clicked on the light and walked in. He closed the door behind him, not wanting to be interrupted as he thoroughly checked the space for clues to what had gone on in Adam's mind.

The room was neat and clean, but this didn't surprise Dillon. There was nothing chaotic or disorganized about Adam the man, or Adam the killer, which is why he hadn't left any clues behind each time he'd murdered or attempted to kill.

The small closet held nothing but clothes and the bathroom held no unexpected surprises. He moved to the chest of drawers and went through each one, carefully checking for false bottoms and underneath each drawer for anything that might be hidden away.

Nothing. He was aware that it was possible he wouldn't find anything. Still, he moved to the nightstand to check those two drawers.

The top drawer held an old Western paperback, a tube of cream for sore muscles and a bottle of pain relief pills. There was also a key chain that held no keys but instead held small long white items.

Curious, Dillon picked it up. He stared at the items dangling from the key chain and then threw it on the bed with horror. One of the skeletons had been missing fingers. He'd just found them.

It shocked him that he'd discovered them, but

what was even more shocking was that Adam had not only kept them but had them in his nightstand.

Far too easily Dillon could visualize the man taking them out of the drawer each night before he went to sleep to relive the murder and mayhem he had caused.

Adam had definitely been a monster. However, acknowledging that didn't scratch the itch Dillon had of wanting to know why and what had happened to turn him into such a heinous killer.

In the second nightstand drawer Dillon found a journal. He flipped through a couple of pages and realized what he had was a chronicle of Adam's life. Hopefully it would hold some answers as to what had turned a young boy into a killer.

He placed the bones in an evidence bag and then carried them and the journal with him back to the house. He handed the evidence bag to Ben, who was seated at the kitchen table waiting for him with several other officers.

"You've got to be kidding me," Ben said as he looked at the bones. "Where did you find them?"

"In his nightstand. I'm assuming you all checked Adam's office in the barn?" he asked.

"We went through it with a fine-tooth comb, but didn't find anything noteworthy," Mike Goodall said. "I figured those fingers had probably gone into the pond with the skull that Dusty fished out."

"I thought the same thing," Dillon admitted.

"Looks like he bleached them," Mike said, revulsion evident in his voice.

"He breached the back door with the ax. Needless to say the door doesn't lock anymore so Cassie will want to have a new one put in as soon as possible," Ben said and then smiled at Dillon. "It's over, Chief. This has all been a monkey on our backs since the day those skeletons were unearthed and now it's finally over."

For the first time Dillon released a deep sigh of relief. The curse of the Holiday ranch had been solved and a murderer was now resting in hell.

Within thirty minutes Dillon was alone in the house. He carried the journal with him up the stairs, but instead of going into his twin bed, he went into Cassie's room.

There was still a jumble of things on the floor, and it didn't take him long to find the photo she'd told him about. The ring was on Adam's finger, the same ring he'd found in the graves. It was now evidence he didn't need, but he would take it into the station tomorrow and put it in the evidence room.

Case closed.

He started to go back to his room, intending to read as much of the journal as he could before sleep overtook him. But instead he turned on the lamp next to Cassie's bed and then turned off the overhead light.

What he wanted more than anything was to sleep in the sheets that smelled of her. He shucked his clothes and got into the bed. He opened the journal, but his thoughts were momentarily filled with Cassie.

He'd sworn to himself that he'd never tell a woman he loved her only to have her leave. He'd been wrong. Tomorrow he intended to tell Cassie that she was the woman he'd been waiting for…the woman he wanted by his side for the rest of his life.

Tomorrow he'd press her for a final decision on whether she was going to leave Bitterroot or stay here with him. He only hoped her answer didn't rip his heart out.

Chapter 16

Cassie awoke suddenly, a gasp escaping her as she left a nightmare behind and came to full consciousness. Faint morning light danced in through the hospital window.

The dream had been visions of reality. Adam had chased her out of the house, swinging the ax as he advanced on her. She'd hidden in the barn and he'd found her and dragged her out of the hay and into the open. Only in her nightmare Dillon hadn't arrived and just as Adam swung the ax, she'd awakened.

Her heartbeat slowed to a more normal pace. Her knee hurt and her body ached, but she was safe. She was finally safe and she'd never felt more free than she did at this very moment.

There was no more danger, no more fear inside

her. The rest of her life stretched out before her as a blank page in a book. All she had to do was decide what she wanted written there.

Did she want to be a rancher in Bitterroot, Oklahoma, who sold paintings on a website? Or did she want to return to an uncertain life in New York City to pursue what Dillon had said and what she knew now was a childish dream?

One thing was clear. It would be terribly difficult to remain here with her love for Dillon so deep and abiding in her heart.

He'd told her he loved her, but he'd also told her he didn't like it. She knew she wasn't the kind of woman he wanted in his life. She'd never be that woman. But she also wouldn't be chased out of town because of any emotional wound left behind by him.

She'd faced off against a killer and she'd come out on the other side. She was strong enough to deal with anything. A peace resonated inside her.

She drifted back to sleep, and when she awakened again it was because her breakfast had arrived. There were scrambled eggs and toast, fresh fruit and several slices of bacon.

"Oh, my gosh, this looks delicious," she said to the woman who had delivered the tray. Her name tag read Rhonda, but Cassie had never met her before.

"You deserve a good breakfast after all you suffered through last night," Rhonda replied. "You're already the talk of the town and it isn't even nine o'clock yet."

Cassie took the lid off a cup of coffee. "I'm just glad it's all over."

"Everyone is glad about that. In fact, there are a bunch of cowboys outside who are eager to see you. Do you want me to send them in a couple at a time?"

"Sure," she replied.

As Rhonda left the room Cassie ran her fingers through her hair in hopes of looking more presentable and then leaned back and took a sip of the coffee.

Sawyer, Brody and Clay were the first ones into the room. They all held their hats in their hands and Sawyer held a vase full of flowers.

"These are for you," he said and set the vase on her bedside table.

"Thank you. They're beautiful," she replied.

"It's good to see you looking okay," Clay said. "We've all been worried sick about you."

"I'm a little battered and bruised, but I'll be all right," she replied, surprised at the rise of emotion in her chest as she gazed at the three men.

"We didn't know," Sawyer said. "Cassie, if we'd known about Adam we would have taken him down ourselves."

"Dammit, we should have known. We grew up with him, but he never let on what demons were inside him," Brody added.

"We would have never let him get close to you if we'd known," Sawyer added with vehemence.

"All's well that ends well," she replied. "I don't want any of you blaming yourselves. Adam hid his demons well, but it's over and now we all go back to business as usual."

For the next hour she assured all the cowboys who had come to visit her that she was fine. By the time they'd all left she had more flowers than she knew what to do with and a renewed love for all the men who worked for her.

However, the beautiful flowers and all the men's good wishes didn't take away from the fact that the one man she'd wanted to see hadn't come to see her.

It was just after two o'clock when Dillon arrived at the hospital. He'd spoken to the doctor and had been told that Cassie would be released as soon as he arrived to take her home.

As much as he'd wanted to see her he'd had official business to take care of that morning. He'd taken the evidence collected into the station to log it into the evidence room and had written up his report as to the events that had occurred the night before.

He'd stayed up most of the night reading Adam's journal and had gotten a much clearer picture of the forces that had worked in Adam's life to turn him into the monster he had become. But even a tragic childhood didn't justify what Adam had ultimately chosen to do.

He now turned down the corridor that would take him to Cassie's room and he couldn't control the leap of his heart when he saw her sitting in a chair next to the window.

"Looks like a flower store in here," he said.

She turned and smiled. "My cowboys went a little overboard. I've already told the nurse to see that the flowers all get distributed to any other patients here."

"I see somebody got you some clothes." She was clad in a pair of blue scrubs. He frowned. "I should have thought to have something from the house brought up to you."

She stood and winced slightly. "It's okay. One of the nurses let me borrow these. I'll bring them back to her tomorrow."

"Your knee is still hurting."

"A little. The doc says I need to come back in about a week from now and he'll take the stitches out. I'm just more than ready to get home. My orders have already been written so I'm free to go."

"Then let's get you home."

Minutes later they were in his car and headed back to the ranch. He wanted to tell her he loved her, but now just didn't seem to be the right time.

"I found a journal in Adam's room," he said.

"Really? Have you read it yet?"

"I spent most of the night reading it." He told her about Adam's mother, who had obviously been a selfish woman who preferred her lovers over her little boy.

"After he killed her and everyone believed she'd run off, Adam's father fell apart. He started drinking and became violent, and after a year Adam ran away."

"And wound up on the ranch with seven other boys," Cassie replied.

Dillon nodded. "He killed them at various intervals for a variety of reasons, but in his mind he was protecting the only woman he thought of as a good and loving mother."

"My aunt Cass."

"After she died and you arrived here he saw you as an angel that belonged to him."

"That's so creepy," she replied as he turned into the ranch's driveway. "He must have spied on us and when he saw me getting closer to you he branded me as the whore who had to die."

"You do realize nothing that happened is your fault," he said. The last thing he wanted was for her to entertain any kind of guilt over Adam's actions.

He parked the car and then went around to help her out. "Somebody fixed the door," she said in surprise.

"I didn't want you coming home to a reminder of what happened. Flint and Mac got a new one this morning and we hung it."

They entered the house and he pointed her to the sofa. "Get comfortable. I intend to wait on you for the rest of the day."

"You don't have to do that," she protested.

"I know, but I want to. Can I get you something to eat? Something to drink?" He watched as she sank down into the sofa cushions. "How about a pillow beneath your knee?" Jeez, this whole conversation felt so inane with his love for her wanting to be shouted.

"I've got it." She took one of the throw pillows

and placed it under her knee. "Why don't you just sit down and talk to me about anything but murder and bad times."

Before he could open his mouth a knock sounded at the back door. Dillon answered to find Halena and Mary Redwing. Halena wore a fancy pink hat and carried a large casserole dish. "I brought dinner," she announced as she set the dish on the kitchen table. "And I wore one of my best hats because it's a good hat day when Cassie survives an evil attack."

"I'm in here," Cassie called.

"We just wanted to stop by and see how you're doing," Mary said as they entered the great room. "Honestly, Cassie, I don't know what this town would do without you. You've been a safe haven for so many people."

"Including us," Halena added.

Dillon knew she was talking about the fact that Cassie had taken in Mary and Halena when a drug dealer wanted to kill them.

Cassie shook her head. "Anybody would have done the same."

"That's not true," Halena protested. "You are a kind and caring woman, Cassie, and you don't realize what a huge asset you are to this town."

Cassie's cheeks dusted a pretty pink. "Stop," she protested. "I'm just hoping nobody is in danger ever again around here."

The two women visited with her a little longer and then Dillon saw them out. "Does she know?" Halena asked him as she stepped out the back door.

"Know what?" he asked.

"You look at her like a man in love," Halena replied.

"I am in love with her," Dillon replied.

"When are you going to tell her? Do you want to borrow a hat to wear?"

Dillon smiled at the old Native American woman. "Thanks, Halena, but I think I'm good."

Throughout the afternoon he tried to get a chance to talk to Cassie, but there was a steady stream of visitors to check up on her.

Even Dusty and Trisha Cahill arrived with Trisha's son, Cooper, and reminded Cassie that if it hadn't been for the safe haven Cassie had provided for Trisha and Cooper when her deadly ex had come after them, who knew what might have happened.

Lucas and Nicolette Taylor also stopped by to check in on Cassie. As the two female friends visited in the great room Dillon and Lucas sat at the kitchen table.

"You have no idea how shocked I am," Lucas said.

"Everyone is shocked," Dillon replied. "Did Adam ever say much about his childhood?"

Lucas frowned. "Just that he didn't get along with his mother and that's why he'd run away from home."

"He killed her when he was fourteen," Dillon said and then went on to tell Lucas what he'd read in Adam's journal.

"You know, all twelve of us men came here with horrible backgrounds, but none of the rest of us turned into killers. I can feel sorry for the boy he was, but that doesn't justify what he did as a man," Lucas replied.

"I know he was from Tulsa so I'm going to try to contact his father to see if he wants to claim his son's body."

"I wouldn't count on it. As far as I know Adam never spoke to his father again after he ran away."

If nobody claimed Adam's body then he would be buried without ceremony in the Bitterroot cemetery.

Finally everyone was gone and it was just the two of them as dusk fell outside. Dillon put Halena's casserole into the oven to warm. He returned to the great room and sank down next to her on the sofa.

"We need to talk," he said.

She sat up as a tiny frown danced across her forehead. "I know. What I don't understand is why you're still here with me. I don't really need any help despite you treating me like an invalid all day. The danger is over and you can finally get back to your own life."

The blue scrubs made her eyes the blue of the Oklahoma sky and he couldn't wait another minute to speak of his love for her. "I don't want to get back to my own life. Cassie, I'm in love with you."

Her frown deepened. "You said that last night before you left here and you also told me you didn't like it."

"I was wrong. You're the woman I want to spend the rest of my life with. I want to wake up with you in my bed every morning and go to sleep with you in my arms."

The words that had been held in for so long exploded out of him. "Cassie, I don't want to be the man who steals any dream from you, but I just wanted to tell you that I've never loved anyone the way I do you."

No joy leaped into her eyes. He'd hoped for that, and his heart took a slow descent in his chest. Instead she looked at him in confusion. "But I'm not the kind of woman you want to love."

"Whoever told you that?" He moved closer to her. "I've always dreamed of falling in love with a strong, brave woman who occasionally smells like turpentine and burns dinner. I've always wanted a woman who has a passion for painting and a passion for me."

He held his breath and watched the play of emotions that danced across her features. Disbelief, hope and finally the joy he'd been hoping for.

"Oh, Dillon, I'm so in love with you." Her lips trembled and he fought the need to cover them with his own.

"But what about New York?" he asked.

"Where? I once had a dream about a city where I could be somebody and find my happiness and then I grew up and put that childish dream behind me. What I want more than anything now is to marry a strong, sexy chief of police who will let me paint and burn dinner and make apple pies that pucker lips. I want a man who will give me babies and stay with me right here on this ranch for the rest of our lives."

It was Dillon's turn to stare at her, hoping—praying—that this wasn't a joke. "For real?"

"For real, and if you don't grab me up in your arms and kiss me right now I'm going to scream," she replied.

He stood and pulled her up and wrapped his arms around her and then slanted his mouth against hers. The kiss held all of the love and the passion he had inside for her.

And she returned it with a heat and welcome that let him know exactly how she felt about him. The kiss ended and he smiled at her.

"I love you, Dillon, but you know you're in for a life you never imagined. I lose track of time when I'm painting. I'll probably never master the art of baking an apple pie and…"

Dillon pressed a finger across her mouth. "There is nothing you can say that will make me stop loving you or wanting you forever." He searched her features for a long moment. "Cassie, more than anything I want you to be happy."

"I've found my happiness, Dillon. I know it sounds crazy but last night as I was running away from Adam, I realized that I am somebody worthwhile and that my place is right here in this town, on this ranch. It's icing on the cake to have you." She grinned. "A huge hunk of gooey chocolate icing that will sustain my happiness for the rest of my life."

He kissed her once again and when the kiss ended

she gazed at him. "If you love me, then take me up-stairs and let's celebrate our love for real," she said, her eyes shining with a happiness that stoked his even higher.

"What about your knee?" he suddenly asked.

"What knee?" She hobbled toward the stairs. "Come on, Chief, don't keep a woman waiting."

He laughed and hurried after her. Yes, he loved this woman with all his heart and soul…and he liked it.

Epilogue

"Are you sure the tables look all right?" Cassie turned and looked at Dillon, who was in the process of filling a huge punch bowl.

"Cassie, the tables look beautiful. Your center-pieces are gorgeous and the day is going to go off without a hitch," he replied.

"I just hope Cookie made enough mashed potatoes. You know how people like their mashed potatoes with their turkey," she fretted.

It was Thanksgiving, and within a half an hour not only would her cowboys be coming into their dining room for a magnificent feast, but also dozens of people she'd invited from town.

The long tables were covered with autumn-colored tablecloths, and Cassie had arranged fresh flowers in vases for each table. The air smelled of turkey and ham and all the trimmings.

Dillon walked over to her and took her hands in his. "Honey, there will be enough mashed potatoes for everyone. There's enough food back in that kitchen to feed the entire county. Cookie even has Sawyer and Flint back there helping him. Now stop worrying and give me a hug."

He didn't have to ask twice. Over the past week she'd learned something new about the man she loved. He was not only passionate, but he was also extremely affectionate.

She wrapped her arms around his waist and smiled up at him. "I have more things to be thankful for this Thanksgiving than ever before in my life."

"I feel the same way," he replied and then captured her lips in a soft, tender kiss.

"Now, that's what I like to see," a male voice called from the doorway.

They broke apart and turned to see Leroy in the doorway, He was dressed in jeans and an orange sweater that sported a huge turkey on the front.

"Don't you look festive," Cassie said as she walked over to greet him.

"Loretta bought me this silly sweater years ago and I figured today was a good day to wear it," he replied. He grinned at Dillon. "I heard you put your place up for sale. Are you two making memories here?"

Dillon threw an arm around Cassie's shoulders. "Absolutely," he replied.

"Then I'm a happy man…and I'm a hungry man," Leroy said.

Cassie laughed. "Find a seat and the food should be coming out soon."

"And maybe I could take just a little turkey home for Boomer?"

"Don't worry, we'll hook you up some goodies to take home," Cassie assured him.

Within minutes the room began to fill up with friends and laughter, and Cookie and his cowboy helpers began to put food on the banquet table.

"There's a rumor going around that you've decided to stay here for good," Halena said to Cassie.

"The rumor is true," Cassie replied and tried to keep her eyes off the hat Halena wore that was bedecked with big autumn leaves and a little stuffed squirrel that looked suspiciously like a dog's toy.

Halena pointed across the room to where Dillon was talking to Dusty and Trisha. "Are you staying for him?"

Cassie smiled. "No, I'm staying for me. I would have chosen to stay here without Dillon. But he is a nice bonus package."

"That he is, and even though you aren't Native American, you are a strong warrior, Cassie, and Bitterroot is happy to have you." To Cassie's surprise the old woman pulled her into a tight hug and then released her.

"And now I believe I'll go torment the men in the kitchen." She left Cassie's side and Cassie headed for the door to greet more of her guests.

When the last of the food was ready, Richard Ainsworth, the mayor of Bitterroot stood to deliver a quick, but nice prayer of thanks.

People were just beginning to form a line to fill their plates when Raymond Humes appeared at the door. A rich anger rose up inside her for the vile man. She knew now what had created the bad blood between him and her aunt Cass. The details had been in her aunt's final journal.

"Raymond, you weren't invited," she said to him, conscious of Dillon coming to stand beside her.

"I thought for sure it was some kind of an oversight. From what I hear we're probably going to be neighbors for a long time, so I thought I'd be welcomed on this day of giving thanks," he said.

"You thought wrong. I don't ever want you on my property again," Cassie replied, not trying to hide her anger.

"You heard the lady, Raymond," Dillon said.

"Wait, on second thought, there is a way I'll let you inside to enjoy the food and company," Cassie said.

"What's that?" Raymond asked curiously.

"Drop your drawers."

Dillon barked a laugh and Raymond stared at her as if she'd lost her mind. "Excuse me?" Raymond sputtered.

"You heard me. Drop your drawers and prove to me that you don't wear the scar of my aunt's bull-whip on your bare butt."

Raymond's face paled and he took a step backward. "I…I don't know what you're talking about."

"Oh, I think you do," Cassie retorted.

"You're as crazy as Cass was," he said as he back-pedaled two more steps.

"And I like that about her," Dillon replied and threw an arm around her shoulder.

Raymond stared at both of them for a long moment and then turned on his heels and stalked away. Cassie turned to Dillon and smiled. "Thank you."

"For what?" he asked.

"For having my back."

He returned her smile. "I'm always going to have your back, Cassie. Now, let's go get a plate and sit down with our friends."

As they stood in line for the food, Cassie's thoughts remained on the journal she had read that had told the tale of a late afternoon when her aunt had gone to the stables. She'd been exhausted from taking care of her dying husband and frightened of what the future held.

And there Raymond had confronted her and tried to rape her. Cass had fought hard and the attempt had been unsuccessful, but before it was all done she had grabbed her bullwhip and snapped it against Raymond's bare butt.

Cassie would be eternally grateful that she hadn't decided to sell the ranch to that despicable man. In fact, she had a heart full of things to be thankful for, especially that she recognized her own worth and knew that just being Cassie was being somebody important.

For the next hour everyone ate too much and laughed together. There was a wonderful sense of community that Cassie cherished.

Cookie, Sawyer and Flint were clearing off the food table to make room for desserts when Dillon's phone rang. He answered and then turned to Cassie.

"That was Annie. I'm needed in town," he said. "I'm sorry, Cassie, but I have to go."

"Don't be sorry. It's your job." Sure, she was disappointed he had to go, but she also knew that loving the chief of police also meant there would be holidays and days off interrupted for official work.

"Walk me out?" he asked.

"Of course." They both got up from the table and left the building.

As soon as they were outside he pulled her into an embrace. "You've created a wonderful Thanksgiving for a lot of people," he said. "And you do know I intend to marry you as soon as possible?"

"Just name the date and I'll be there," she replied.

"I love you, Cassie," he said and took her lips with his in a kiss that spoke of his love for her.

When the kiss ended she gave him a little shove in the chest. "Go, you have a job to do."

"I'll get back here as soon as possible," he replied. "Now, get back inside before you freeze."

Cassie nodded and walked back into the dining room. She stopped in the doorway, stunned by the fact that everyone wore a birthday hat, and balloons had magically appeared to fill every corner of the room.

"Surprise!" everyone yelled.

She turned around to see if Dillon was still there, but he'd disappeared from her view. It wasn't her birthday, but she knew Dillon had arranged this. He didn't know that her birthday was tomorrow. All he'd known was that her birthday was around Thanksgiving and she'd never had a birthday party.

Emotions swelled so big in her chest she couldn't move or speak. Dillon came out of the kitchen carrying a large cake filled with candles and everyone began to sing "Happy Birthday." And then she was laughing and crying at the same time.

Above the glow of the candles Dillon's face was filled with love and happiness. She blew out the candles and when he set down the cake she flew into his arms amid hoots and hollers.

"I'm going to love you like you've never been loved for the rest of our lives," she whispered into his ear.

"Back at you," he replied.

"You asked me once if I believed in soul mates. I do, Dillon, and I know you're mine."

His eyes said it all—they were filled with his love. He released her. "Now, let's eat some cake," he said to everyone.

Cassie sat back down in her chair and looked

around, her heart full. These were her friends and she knew without a doubt she would be happy growing old here. She would paint, she would ranch and she would love Dillon for the rest of her life. And hopefully soon they would begin to build a family and continue the legacy of the Holiday ranch and Aunt Cass.

* * * * *

Don't forget previous titles in the
COWBOYS OF HOLIDAY RANCH *series:*

OPERATION COWBOY DADDY
COWBOY AT ARMS
COWBOY UNDER FIRE
COWBOY OF INTEREST
A REAL COWBOY

Join Britain's BIGGEST Romance Book Club

- **EXCLUSIVE offers every month**
- **FREE delivery direct to your door**
- **NEVER MISS a title**
- **EARN Bonus Book points**

Call Customer Services
0844 844 1358*

or visit
millsandboon.co.uk/subscriptions

* This call will cost you 7 pence per minute plus your phone company's price per minute access charge.

B3